You are cordially invited to the Surprise Wedding
of Ex-Libris Bookstore owner Amanda Bradley
and Heartbreak Saloon keeper William "Dev" Devlin.

Time: Sunday afternoon
Place: Heartbreak Saloon

Join Shelly and Connor O'Rourke
and all of Millionaire, Montana, as we celebrate the
sacred, albeit swift, union of Main Street's much-loved
contenders—er, couple—as they begin their married
and family life together.

(Special attention should be paid to one
Louise Pearson, stuffed-shirt social worker
seeking to expose Dev and Amanda's marriage
as a means to keep Liza, Caleb, Patrick and Betsy
in the family fold.)

Harlequin American Romance presents MILLIONAIRE, MONTANA,
where twelve lucky souls have won a multimillion-dollar jackpot.

Dear Reader,

Welcome to another wonderful month at Harlequin American Romance. You'll notice our covers have a brand-new look, but rest assured that we still have the editorial you know and love just inside.

What a lineup we have for you, as reader favorite Muriel Jensen helps us celebrate our 20th Anniversary with her latest release. *That Summer in Maine* is a beautiful tale of a woman who gets an unexpected second chance at love and family with the last man she imagines. And author Sharon Swan pens the fourth title in our ongoing series MILLIONAIRE, MONTANA. You won't believe what motivates ever-feuding neighbors Dev and Amanda to take a hasty trip to the altar in *Four-Karat Fiancée*.

Speaking of weddings, we have two other tales of marriage this month. Darlene Scalera pens the story of a jilted bride on the hunt for her disappearing groom in *May the Best Man Wed*. (Hint: the bride may just be falling for her husband-to-be's brother.) Dianne Castell's *High-Tide Bride* has a runaway bride hiding out in a small town where her attraction to the local sheriff is rising just as fast as the flooding river.

So sit back and enjoy our lovely new look and the always-quality novels we have to offer you this—and every—month at Harlequin American Romance.

Best Wishes,

Melissa Jeglinski
Associate Senior Editor
Harlequin American Romance

FOUR-KARAT FIANCÉE
Sharon Swan

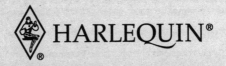

HARLEQUIN®

TORONTO • NEW YORK • LONDON
AMSTERDAM • PARIS • SYDNEY • HAMBURG
STOCKHOLM • ATHENS • TOKYO • MILAN • MADRID
PRAGUE • WARSAW • BUDAPEST • AUCKLAND

Special thanks and acknowledgment are given to
Sharon Swan for her contribution to the
MILLIONAIRE, MONTANA series.

For Muriel, Leah, Charlotte, Bonnie and Karen,
who made doing this story so special

And for Melissa Jeglinski, who brought us together
creating a town to remember

RECYCLED PAPER · RECYCLED PAPER

ISBN 0-373-16966-3

FOUR-KARAT FIANCÉE

ABOUT THE AUTHOR

Born and raised in Chicago, Sharon Swan once dreamed of dancing for a living. Instead, she surrendered to life's more practical aspects, settled for an office job, concentrated on typing and being a Chicago Bears fan. Sharon never seriously considered writing a career until she moved to the Phoenix area and met Pierce Brosnan at a local shopping mall. It was a chance meeting that changed her life because she found herself thinking, what if? What if two fictional characters had met the same way? That formed the basis for her next novel, and she's now cheerfully addicted to writing contemporary romance and playing what if?

Sharon loves to hear from readers. You can write to her at P.O. Box 21324, Mesa, AZ 85277.

Books by Sharon Swan

HARLEQUIN AMERICAN ROMANCE

912—COWBOYS AND CRADLES
928—HOME-GROWN HUSBAND*
939—HUSBANDS, HUSBANDS…EVERYWHERE!*
966—FOUR-KARAT FIANCÉE

*Welcome to Harmony

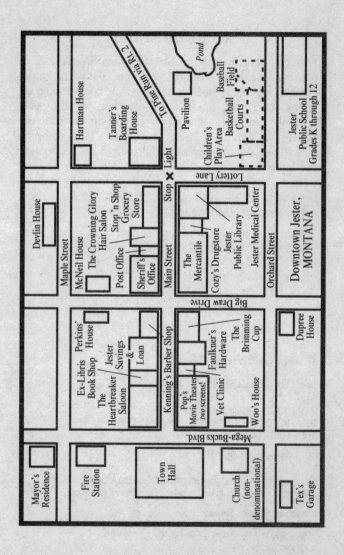

Downtown Jester, MONTANA

Prologue

Maybe he should just grab her up and kiss her.

William Devlin fisted his gloved hands at his sides and debated the merits of that plan. At least, he thought, it would keep Amanda Bradley quiet for a while. It was hard to believe that most folks in Jester, Montana, considered this woman a prime example of a real lady. Then again, she wasn't tearing into most of Jester's small population on a regular basis. Only him.

For two years, ever since she'd opened her fancy bookstore in the same building that was home to his saloon, he'd been treated to complaints about his business. And for the past six months, with some hard-earned savings in hand at last, he'd been offering to buy her share of the old, sprawling building so he could finally have some peace. Too bad it didn't look as if he were getting any, because she kept turning him down flat.

"So I'm asking for the umpteenth time what you intend to do about the constant commotion." Amanda huffed out the words as she shoved her hands into the pockets of her camelhair coat.

Dev tugged the wide brim of his tan Stetson down

a notch and reined in his temper, barely. More griping was the last thing he needed on a snowy January evening cold enough to freeze a man's blood in his veins. What had made him think that he wanted to take a walk anyway? Two steps out of the Heartbreaker Saloon and he'd found himself being confronted by Amanda's righteous indignation right in the middle of Main Street. Again.

"Look, bars aren't the quietest places in the world, but I told you I'd try to keep a lid on things," he replied with all the reasonableness he could muster. Despite his efforts, the words came out gruff. Hell, he used to have a talent for sweet-talking a woman. And he still did, Dev told himself.

Any woman but this one.

Every now and then he'd look at her and forget that she was one ornery female—because she wasn't bad-looking, he had to admit. She was...*petite*, he guessed was the word, with a neat and trim figure that could draw a man's glance. And there was no denying that the long, light brown hair she usually held back with a shiny clip at the nape of her neck had a glossy sheen to it. Her oval face, straight little nose and clear brown eyes were attractive enough to win some notice, as well.

But it was her mouth that for some reason fascinated him.

"I know what you told me," she said, putting a swift end to his reflections, "and just this afternoon two of your patrons almost came to blows right in front of my store."

"Probably a slight difference of opinion," he muttered, lifting a broad shoulder clad in a sheepskin-lined suede jacket. Being put on the defensive didn't please him one blasted bit.

"Humph." She raised her chin another haughty level. "I don't suppose the drinks they downed at your bar had anything to do with it, *Mr. Macho.*"

He had nearly had it. It irritated him no end when she used that nickname she'd come up with for him, one that typically had him retaliating with a private nickname of his own. In another minute, he thought, he'd be locking his lips with hers. And it would be in pure desperation.

"Look, *Ms. Prim,* as I've explained to you Lord knows how many times, I run a—"

Just then a shout rang out, halting him in midsentence. "We won! Dev, we won!"

He whipped around and saw Dean Kenning hopping up and down on the street outside his barbershop less than a block away, as though the snow-covered asphalt had turned to hot bricks. Beside him, two of Dean's longtime cronies, bundled against the cold, watched with stunned expressions as their friend did a jig worthy of a man far younger than the barber's sixty-plus years.

"What in the world—" Dev started to say. Then he remembered it was Tuesday, the day the Big Draw Lottery numbers were announced on Channel 4 right after the evening news. Fifteen states participated, including Montana, and he was one of a dozen hopefuls who contributed a weekly dollar to Jester's private lottery pool—money the other players forked over to the jovial, ruddy-faced barber so he could purchase tickets for their group at the nearby town of Pine Run. They'd won enough in the past few years to celebrate in a small way, but Dean had never done a jig before. Had they finally lucked out?

Dev took off at a fast clip, vaguely aware of Amanda's footsteps hurrying along behind him. A second-story window over one of the stores lining the street flew open. "Land sakes, what's all the commotion about?" a woman asked in a near squeal.

Ignoring that question, the barber kept right on shouting. "We won!"

"What do you mean we won?" Dev shouted back as he skidded to a halt in front of the barbershop.

At last Dean stopped jumping around and held up a small piece of paper. "These are the jackpot numbers I just wrote down. And one of tickets I bought for us matches all of them."

Dev swallowed, hard. "Are you sure?"

"I'll read them to you," Dean told him, his voice beginning to shake as he handed over the ticket.

In the dim light of an old turn-of-the-century streetlamp, Dev checked the printed computer numbers against those the barber quickly read off. And they matched, every…single…one.

"We *did* win," Dev said in a rough whisper, feeling as though the bottom had dropped right out of his stomach. Looking up, he saw that a small crowd had gathered, and it wasn't long before a woman wedged her way through.

"Let me see that," Shelly Dupree said.

Dev gave the ticket to Shelly, who was another regular in the lottery pool. Over the past few years, the Main Street coffee-shop owner with a ready smile for her customers had become a friend of his. Shelly was also a close friend to Amanda Bradley, he knew, but he'd never held that against her.

"Read them again, Dean," Shelly told the barber. "Slowly."

Dean followed instructions, and moments later Shelly lifted her gaze. Her mouth opened, but no sound came out.

"How much did you win?" someone in the crowd asked.

The barber raised his hands to the dark sky above him, as if he were trying to touch heaven, and looking as though he had. "Forty! Million! Dollars!"

Forty million, was all Dev could think. "That's..." Using a knack for math that had served him well in business, he divided the winning amount twelve ways and soon came up with a figure. "Three million, three hundred and thirty-three thousand, three hundred and...well, you know. One of those numbers with threes that go on forever."

Someone else brought up the fact that taxes would have to be paid, but Dev was hardly going to carp about that at this point. "We'll still be millionaires!" he declared with a wide grin. *A millionaire...a millionaire.* The words echoed in his mind.

Years ago, when he was growing up in Jester, more than a few folks had never expected him to amount to much, not coming from the no-account family he undeniably had. Once, defiant of their judgment, he'd played the bad boy to the hilt, until he'd turned thirty and decided it was time to try to make something of himself—something Jester's citizens could respect. So he'd left behind the days after high school when he couldn't wait for his shift to end at his first real job at the slaughterhouse in Pine Run, followed by the years when he'd amused himself in the role of wise-guy bartender at the Heartbreaker Saloon. Instead, he'd scraped up enough cash to buy his uncle's run-down bar and through sheer hard work had made it a consistently profitable operation.

And now he wasn't only a successful businessman. He was a *millionaire*.

Elated, Dev turned to the woman standing beside him and lifted her right off the ground. With a secure grip on a slender waist, he waltzed her around in a wide circle as thick, white flakes rained down on them, holding her close and feeling the length of her petite body snug against his.

And then he realized who that petite body belonged to and set her down in a hurry.

Amanda Bradley stared up at him, eyes wide. She didn't look anywhere near as jubilant as he felt, Dev noted as he took a swift step back. Then again, she'd never contributed to the weekly pool and wasn't one of the big winners. Not like he was.

Dev's own gaze narrowed in speculation at the thought that maybe he had enough money at last to buy her part of the building they shared. Maybe he'd no longer have to rue the day his uncle had sold that piece of property to her parents long ago. Maybe, just maybe, he could make her an offer she couldn't refuse and finally get some peace.

But all at once her gaze narrowed, too, as though she'd read his mind. He was sure of it when she issued soft words for his ears alone that nonetheless rang with conviction.

"Never in a million years," Amanda told him, looking him straight in the eye.

And Dev knew that, despite his unbelievably good fortune, he still had his work cut out for him.

Chapter One

Never in a million years, she'd told him. Amanda recalled that ringing statement on a cloudy April afternoon, thinking that she had been as good as her word.

Dev Devlin might now be a wealthy man, especially in comparison to most of Jester's far-from-affluent residents, but she hadn't given in to him one inch. Winter had bowed to spring and her quiet bookstore still shared a building with his busy bar—something that continued to rub both parties the wrong way, even though Main Street hadn't seen a real confrontation between them since the town sheriff had actually stepped in to break up the last one several weeks earlier. Although neither had declared an end to hostilities, the two of them seemed to have struck up a wary truce. Which was just as well, Amanda told herself, because at the moment she had something more important than her problems with the Heartbreak Saloon's owner to consider.

She had the fate of four children to think about and worry over. Four young kids who had lost their father and mother.

Four orphans she'd only recently discovered existed.

But she couldn't think about them now. At the moment she had to keep her mind on business, Amanda knew, because today problems had also cropped up at the Ex-Libris, her bookstore.

"What do you plan to do with all this new stock?" Irene Caldwell asked. A widow in her early sixties, Irene was a big reader and faithful Ex-Libris customer who also took on the role of occasional, and very able, helper at the bookstore whenever the need arose.

Amanda braced her elbows on the store's dark mahogany front counter and studied a copy of *Midnight Passions,* one of many filling several cartons stacked on the dove gray carpet that stretched the length of the high-ceilinged room. The hardcover novel featured a dusky rose cover slashed with bold ebony letters that left little doubt as to its sexy subject matter.

"Most of the books will be shipped back to the distributor's warehouse, since I made it plain enough to them over the phone that I didn't order a *hundred* copies." Amanda blew out a breath. "The manager I talked to wasn't overjoyed at the news, but I told him he was getting them back, regardless."

Casting another look around, Irene shook a head topped by graying hair worn in an upswept style and slid her hands into the front pockets of her navy wool cardigan. "How many did you order?"

"Ten, and I'm not even sure I can sell all of those. A display will stir some interest, but sales remain to be seen."

"Hmm. Well, it probably wouldn't hurt you to take home a copy," Irene said with a twinkle in her eye.

That had Amanda smiling a faint smile despite everything. "Figure it will put me in the mood for a man…and possibly marriage?" Which, she knew, would please the older woman no end. Having had a happy marriage of her own, Irene would undoubtedly have little objection to seeing the world's entire adult population pair off into loving couples pursuing a lifetime of wedded bliss.

"I must confess that romance seems to be in the air lately," Irene said, eyes still twinkling. "First Shelly Dupree stopped running the coffee shop long enough to fall for Jester's handsome new doctor, Connor O'Rourke. Then Jack Hartman finally took a good look at Melinda Woods, after which the two vets decided to share more than a practice. And then, just recently, Luke McNeil, who's always been an excellent sheriff but needed more in his life than law enforcement, reconciled with his long-ago sweetheart, Jennifer Faulkner."

"Mmm," was the most neutral comment Amanda could offer. Despite Irene's theory, all she smelled in the air was the fragrant jar of potpourri she'd set beside the cash register.

"You probably wouldn't still be single yourself," Irene pointed out, "if you had encouraged one of the nice boys you dated before you went off to college— or one of the nice men who asked you out when you came back to Jester."

But none of those boys she'd shared popcorn with at Pop's Movie Theatre—or the men whose dinner invitations she'd mostly declined since her return to Montana nearly three years earlier—had been right, not for her. And while, as the child of divorced parents, she might not believe quite as much in happily ever after as Irene did, Amanda couldn't deny that she hoped to find Mr. Right someday—a man who just might sweep her off her feet and send her pulse leaping.

Which is exactly what happened four months ago on a snowy January night.

No, Amanda quickly countered in response to that sudden thought. It was just the excitement of the moment.

Unfortunately her more candid side knew that wasn't the total truth of the matter. Dev Devlin, for all that he irritated her, was an attractive man. Dark blond hair the color of ripening wheat. Deep blue eyes that echoed a Western summer sky. Six feet tall and well-muscled.

Yes, he was quite a sight.

He'd also, however, been more than wild enough in his younger days to have her sure he'd never really settle down. And that alone made him the wrong man for her—because, for all that she valued her independence, she was also a settling-down kind of woman. Deep down, she wanted the kind of marriage Irene felt everyone was entitled to, and that meant waiting for the *right* man.

Just then the heavy mahogany door sporting a gleaming glass center opened and Finn Hollis stepped in from the sidewalk. Thin and lanky, with a full head of white hair, the retired librarian was another of Jester's big lottery winners and had become one of the bookstore's best customers, too, during the past few months. Finn, however, seldom wanted any of the books Amanda had in stock. No, the widower with a slew of children and grandchildren to keep him happily occupied had acquired a passion for collecting rare books, as well. Which usually meant a profit for the store, but could also mean putting some real effort into tracking down the items on Finn's latest list.

And unless she was mistaken, Amanda mused, the folded piece of white stationery Finn currently held in one large, lined hand was yet another order to be filled.

"Hello, ladies," Finn said in his normal courteous fashion.

Unlike some of Jester's residents, the man who owned a sprawling farmhouse north of town didn't favor Western-style garb. Instead, his tweed jackets and dark trousers implied a more scholarly bent, and Finn did seem to be a font of knowledge on many subjects. Amanda had pitted her brain against his more than once, and despite receiving good enough grades to earn a scholarship to a small yet well-respected college in the Pacific Northwest, she'd seldom bested him. Now she managed to greet him with her second smile of the day, although the nagging worries she couldn't quite set aside made it a halfhearted effort.

In contrast, Irene's own wide version looked far more enthusiastic. And amused. "Don't tell me you're ordering more books, Finn Hollis."

His gaze took on a sheepish glint behind wire-rimmed glasses. "I can't seem to help myself."

Amanda studied the list he'd handed over. As she'd expected, none of the titles would be simple to find. She'd have to spend several hours at the store's computer this afternoon just to make a respectable start. "It's a good thing you have a big home," she told him.

"Still, if you're not careful, you'll find yourself up to your ears in the printed word," Irene tacked on with dry humor.

"That's why I've decided to add on a library

wing," Finn informed the two women. "I suppose if Dev Devlin can build an entire house, and a large one at that, I can indulge my hobby."

When both her companions slid sidelong glances her way, Amanda knew they'd be far from surprised if she offered a caustic comment in response, not considering what had probably taken on the dimensions of a local feud—or a battle royal between the sexes. But she just wasn't up to it. Not today.

"I understand the new Devlin house will have six bedrooms," Finn added after a moment.

"My goodness," Irene said. "What would a single man need with a half dozen bedrooms?"

"Maybe he plans to fill them with willing women," Amanda suggested, just a bit archly. No one, not even her, would argue the fact that the Heartbreaker Saloon's owner had a longstanding reputation as a ladies' man. "He must be getting tired of entertaining his, ah, women friends in the back room he's living in behind the bar."

"He doesn't seem to have, er, entertained anyone for quite a while," Finn confided in a low murmur, proving that even Jester's most scholarly resident wasn't opposed to a bit of gossip. "Not from what I've heard, that is."

And where he'd heard it was at Dean Kenning's barbershop. Amanda was all but positive of that. Finn and Dean were still great cronies, even though Henry Faulkner, their longtime friend, had recently passed away.

"Well, it hardly matters to me," she said. "I don't care who the man in question entertains as long as he does it *quietly.*"

Irene and Finn exchanged a look at the pointed tone

of that last word. "Yes, well, I have to go," the older woman wasted no time in saying, as though afraid that, if the female half of the battle of the sexes got started on the subject of the male half, the shaky truce Amanda suspected many were watching with interest might collapse—just as the picnic pavilion at Jester Community Park had strangely collapsed last month, prompting an ongoing sheriff's investigation.

"I believe I have to leave, too," Finn said. "I appreciate your getting those books for me, Amanda."

And with that, they both were gone, leaving the Ex-Libris's owner to her own devices. The proud owner, Amanda couldn't deny, aiming her gaze around the front of her store. With its wide display window containing an attractive assortment of current literature and its walls covered by tall mahogany bookshelves backed by flocked wallpaper featuring a delicate lilac stripe, it was as classy a place as she'd been able to make it—right down to the lilting notes of the "Violin Masters" CD that currently played softly in the background.

Only the shipping cartons stacked everywhere marred the scene. If they weren't picked up tomorrow, she would make another call and be even more blunt if she had to about expecting them to be taken back. She hadn't spent several years after college working for a major bookselling chain in Seattle for nothing. She could get things accomplished.

In fact, she'd risen to the position of assistant manager before concluding that big-city life didn't really suit her. What she wanted was a bookstore of her own in the small town she thought of as home. So she'd come back with her hard-earned savings in hand, and now, at the age of thirty, she had more than enough experience behind her to get things done.

In the business world, at any rate. There was still, Amanda knew, the fate of four young children to consider. And there, she was far from sure how much she could do.

She only knew she had to try.

BY THE TIME Amanda put the gracefully scribed Closed sign in the front window at six o'clock, she wanted nothing more than to go home and soak in a hot tub. Even beyond that, she knew what she needed was the good night's sleep she'd failed to get for the past several evenings. Maybe, she mused as she tallied the day's receipts, taking something with her to read besides the intricate mystery she was currently in the middle of would help. And with that thought, her gaze landed on the copy of *Midnight Passions* still resting at one side of the counter.

Why not? she asked herself. It would indeed be something different, and that could be just what she needed to relax a bit.

What Amanda didn't want, and her nerves certainly didn't need, was to catch sight of one of the Heartbreaker Saloon's patrons weaving his way toward her as she left the Ex-Libris at just after six-thirty. She recognized Guy Feldon. He was one of the people who had followed hard on the heels of Jester's newfound wealth.

"Millionaire, Montana," was how the press had dubbed a place little more than a pinpoint on the state map, and the town had been flooded with reporters. Thankfully, the relentless press coverage seemed to have died down, although some residents' private business was still being leaked to the media. More than a few of Jester's citizens suspected that one of their own was acting as informer, but no one really knew who was responsible.

The burly man currently approaching with unsteady steps wasn't with the media, however. No, Guy Feldon appeared to be basically an opportunist who wouldn't hesitate to take advantage of another's good fortune. He usually played the part of the lazy drifter, but more than one person had remarked on spying a cunning glint in his eye.

Now his gaze was trained on Amanda, and she by no means liked what she saw in it. When it raked her from head to toe, even the fact that most of her body was covered by the classic wide folds of her beige raincoat brought little comfort.

"Well, hi, sugar pie," Feldon drawled, his speech slurred.

Sugar pie? Amanda's teeth clenched in response. It didn't take a genius, she thought, to see that she was headed for trouble. Or, rather, trouble was headed for her.

"Cat got your tongue?" Feldon came to a wavering halt right in front of her. "Have to say I envy it if it does." His mouth curved in a leer.

"I'd appreciate it if you'd get out of my way," Amanda replied with brisk directness. Living in a big city had taught her the value of maintaining a firm front in an environment where crime was an unfortunate fact of life. One of the benefits of returning to Jester was that she never so much as felt uneasy walking alone on an empty street—never until now.

"Too bad I'm of no mind to step aside." Feldon leaned in. Even in the dimness of a twilight sky, his face looked nearly as flushed as the red checks on his flannel jacket. "I might be persuaded, though, if you gave me a sample of what I'm missing."

You should live so long, Amanda reflected with disgust. She took a better grip on the book she held, hitched her sleek shoulder bag higher, and prepared to move on. "If you don't let me pass, I'm turning around and heading to the sheriff's office."

Feldon's hand snaked out to grab her arm. "I don't think so," he muttered, his expression suddenly as dark as his shaggy black hair.

Amanda knew it was too late to run. But she could shout for help, she decided even as another large hand came up to cup her chin hard enough to keep her lips clamped shut.

"Maybe I'll just take, since you don't feel like giving," Feldon said, leaning closer, then closer still. Amanda did her best to struggle, but he was almost twice her size. Her pulse began to pound as all-out panic threatened.

And then he was yanked right away from her by someone who stared daggers at Guy Feldon from under the wide brim of a tan Stetson before sending the burly man lurching into the street with a well-placed fist to the jaw.

For once, Amanda was actually glad to see Dev Devlin.

A few people poked their heads outside at that point, as if just aware that something was up on Main Street. Amanda took note of it with a quick glance around her even as most of her attention remained fixed on the two men steps away.

"Come on, Feldon," Dev said in a near growl, his

fists still clenched. "Let's see you take on someone more your size."

"Damned if I won't," the other man shot back.

Amanda watched what happened next, thinking that it was like a scene straight out of an action movie. Fists flew with abandon and several grunts were exchanged when they found their target, but it wasn't long before a clear victor emerged as Dev sent his opponent flying with a particularly solid punch.

"More?" he asked after taking a few rapid strides forward to stand over the burly man sprawled in the street.

Feldon looked up. "I'm done."

"Well then, so are we," Dev said, "unless the lady wants you dragged over to the sheriff's place so she can press charges."

Mindful that several people had gathered for a closer look at the fight, Amanda shook her head. She still wanted nothing more than to go home.

Dev brushed his palms on his snug-fitting Levi's and reached up to tap his hat down lower on his forehead. "Looks like you're getting off easy," he told his opponent as he shoved his hands into the pockets of his brown leather jacket. "I suggest you haul yourself up—and think about leaving town while you're at it, because I've just decided that this place isn't big enough for the both of us."

Feldon mumbled what might have been a curse, then got to his feet and beat a swift retreat.

After watching him disappear around a corner, Dev looked at Amanda. "Are you all right?"

Vaguely aware of other voices echoing that question, she dipped her head in a nod and kept her gaze on the man walking toward her. The truth was that after everything that had happened that day and all she had on her mind, she found herself close to tears. Nevertheless, her pride had her determined not to shed any before an audience.

"Thank you," she said, gazing into the deep blue eyes of the Heartbreaker Saloon's owner. For coming to my rescue, she could have added, and didn't. It was startling to realize that the person she'd been at odds with for so long had done exactly that.

He studied her, taking in what she hoped was at least a somewhat calm expression. She knew he wasn't fooled by the way he frowned. "If you're on your way home, I'll walk you there."

"That's not necessary," she assured him.

"Whether it is or not, I'm doing it," he countered.

Too tired to mount a real protest, Amanda surrendered with another nod. The irony of it wasn't lost on her. Who would have ever thought she'd give in to this man on anything? she asked herself. And did this mark a change in their relationship?

Something told her that just might be the case as she issued an absent goodbye to the people gathered around and fell into step beside him.

Dev's blood gradually cooled as he concentrated on shortening his stride to match his companion's. Their footsteps tapped out a slow rhythm as they walked down a darkening street. There was no point in wondering whether he should have kicked Feldon's butt for good measure, he told himself. Hopefully, the jerk would take the advice he'd been given and leave town. If not, Dev vowed to personally see to it.

He might be a successful businessman—he might be a *millionaire*—but he could still get a dirty job done if necessary. This evening's brawl had proved that. He hadn't lost the knack of putting his fists to good use. Except these days he knew when to back off. Seeing Amanda Bradley safely home had been more important than continuing to pound on the man who'd been forcing himself on her.

A man who'd had more to drink than he should have at the Heartbreaker, Dev's conscience reminded him.

He frowned in response, thinking that if someone was known to be driving, he and the two bartenders working for him didn't hesitate to shut them off or take car keys away. But how the hell was anyone supposed to know that a man—a *customer*—would practically assault a woman steps from the saloon's doorstep?

Sure, the Heartbreaker's male regulars could get rowdy at times. But assault a female? No way. Most of them would have liked nothing better than to pound on Feldon themselves, given the chance. So instead of letting guilt nag at him over what had happened, Dev figured everyone would be better off if he just tried to do his damnedest to make sure it never happened again.

"Nice night for a stroll down Mega Bucks Boulevard," he said in a bid to make conversation.

Amanda glanced up at him and spoke for the first time since they'd started their walk. "Do you find our mayor's habit of renaming streets since the lottery win to be as bizarre as I do?"

The question, while straightforward enough, was issued in a softer tone than Dev was accustomed to hearing from the Ex-Libris's owner—who, he remembered, had informed him somewhat haughtily during one of their go-rounds that the store's name came from a Latin phrase that loosely translated meant "from the books." And it was just as well she *had* told him, because he knew he'd have never figured that one out.

He lifted one shoulder in a shrug. "Can't see how renaming a few streets hurts anything."

Jester's mayor, Bobby Larson, had also been touting the idea of building a hotel on land now dedicated to the community park, and Dev was less sure how he felt about that plan. The one thing he was dead certain of was a definite desire to avoid town politics. He had plenty of other things to occupy him.

Such as his house, he thought as they crossed Maple Street, where the new Devlin residence would soon reach the move-in stage. He'd been headed there for the daily check he made on it when he'd found himself trading blows with Guy Feldon instead.

"Were you hurt in that fight?" Amanda asked, as though she'd caught the direction his thoughts had taken.

"No." He had no intention of whining about a few aches and pains. "What have you got there?" he asked, changing the subject as he glanced down at the book she held tightly to her. All he could make out were the edges of a dusky rose cover.

"Oh." She hesitated a moment. "It's, ah, a novel, just something I thought I'd try."

"Something different than you usually read?"

Again she paused. "Well, let's just say it's a change from what I've been reading lately."

Her reply was just vague enough to have him wishing he could get a better look at that book. Maybe it would tell him more about the woman he'd come to think of as a thorn in his side. He still believed the best thing he could do was buy her part of the building they shared. He could even knock down the wall separating their properties, make a few changes to spruce up the bar area and expand his business—which was thriving, if he did say so himself.

Her business was another story, he more than suspected. If it weren't for the pastries usually on hand in a sitting area at the back of the bookstore, along with tea served in fancy cups to wash down a helping of the local news of the day, how many customers would regularly visit the place? Probably not enough to turn a healthy profit. If only he could convince her to sell out to him.

They arrived at Amanda's one-story white frame house in a matter of minutes. Dev took note of the fact that although it was a long way from new, it appeared well cared for. It was a far cry from the run-down house he'd grown up in on the outskirts of town, that was for sure. This place looked…*homey,* he guessed was the word, with its front yard enclosed by a short picket fence and what seemed to be, judging by what he could make out in the light coming from a nearby streetlamp, a circle of dried lavender decorating the plain wood door.

"I'll wait until you get in before I take off," he told her when they reached the covered front porch.

"All right." She retrieved a key ring from her shoulder bag and opened the door, then switched on an inside light and turned back to him. "Thank you again for…" Stopping in midsentence, she stared up at him, her gaze narrowing. "You *are* hurt. There's blood on your lip."

That came as no surprise, since he'd started tasting it when they were halfway to her place. "It's nothing," he said.

"It's something," she replied with a trace of the brisk tone he more often associated with her. "Come in and let me have a look at it."

He thought about declining. But it could be he'd get another opportunity to bring up the subject of buying her out. Deciding to take his chances, he said, "Okay," and let her lead him into the house.

The inside seemed as homey as the outside, Dev concluded with a glance around the living room. Again everything looked far from new, but it also looked comfortable, even cozy—a lot cozier, certainly, than anywhere he'd ever lived.

Amanda laid the book she'd been carrying on a small end table and propped her leather shoulder bag on top of it. "Take off your jacket and have a seat," she told him as she switched on a short brass lamp. "I'll be right back with a washcloth and the first aid kit."

He obeyed orders, tossed both his jacket and hat on an overstuffed moss-green chair and sat down on a plump flowered sofa. His gaze was drawn to a photo standing on a narrow wood wall shelf, one he recognized as a shot of a younger Amanda with her mother, who he recalled had passed away about ten years earlier after a short illness. By then, Amanda's father had long since left town, and under circumstances no one living in Jester at the time had probably forgotten.

Dev leaned his head against the back on the sofa and waited for his hostess to return, then waited some more before he finally began to wonder if something was wrong. Could she be the one who was really injured? After all, she'd been putting up a considerable struggle when he'd yanked Feldon away from her.

She might not appreciate his roaming around her

place, but he was going to check on her anyway, he decided. If she got teed off, well she'd been teed off at him plenty already.

Dev got up and started down a narrow hallway toward the rear of the house. Off to one side, he saw light spilling through an open doorway. Not about to stop now, he kept going and soon poked his head in what turned out to be a small bathroom. There, he found Amanda standing at the sink with thin tears running down her cheeks.

She jumped when she spotted him. "I was coming back in a minute," she said, brushing the tears away. Her face had gone nearly as pale as the high-necked white blouse she wore with pleated wool trousers.

"If that jerk hurt you, I'll see he pays for it." It was as firm a promise as Dev could make it. God, he hated to see a woman cry. He'd rather take a solid punch in the chest.

Amanda shook her head. "No, he didn't hurt me. I'm fine, really." She sighed. "It's just…been a long day."

Which it may have been, Dev allowed, but he didn't think that was all of it. If Amanda Bradley could hold her own with him—and she had on many occasions— it was hard to believe she'd wind up teary-eyed unless there was a damn good reason for it. Not, he reminded himself, that it was any of his business.

He leaned against the doorjamb and folded his arms across the twin front pockets of his denim shirt. "Want to patch me up now?"

Sighing again, this time in what might have been relief that he hadn't pressed the subject, she nodded and reached up to open the mirrored medicine cabinet.

"As long as you're here, why don't you wash the blood off first?"

He did, making quick work of cleaning the cut at a corner of his lower lip. Then he propped a hip against the sink and let her fuss over him. As close as they were, he couldn't help but catch a whiff of the subtle floral scent coming from the person whose pink-tinged mouth, currently pursed in concentration, continued to fascinate him. As to why it fascinated him, he still hadn't figured that one out.

Right now he did his best to ignore the fact that they were standing a scant inch from each other, telling himself that he'd been without a woman for too long if certain parts of him could even threaten to get stirred up at a time like this. Then the sting of the antiseptic regained his full attention in a hurry.

"Sorry," she said at his brief flinch.

"No problem."

The job was done and they were back in the living room in a matter of moments. It was time to take off, Dev knew. Trouble was, the remembered sight of those tears was still eating at him.

"Look," he said as he reached down for his jacket, "I know it's flat-out none of my concern, but probably no one knows better than I do that for a small person, you can also be a pretty tough one when your back's up. To get as upset as you obviously were a few minutes ago, something more than a long day has to be behind it."

Her gaze met his. "As you said, it's none of your…" Her voice trailed off as the starch suddenly seemed to go right out of her. She walked over to the sofa and sank onto a plump cushion. "I just need some sleep," she murmured—more to herself than to him, it seemed, as though she were talking out loud. "I can't keep tossing and turning night after night."

He set his jacket down again. "Sounds like you've got things on your mind."

She glanced at him and exhaled a short breath. "You could say so."

Maybe her store was doing even worse than he'd figured. That was all he could come up with. And if that was the problem, he knew he could offer her a quick solution. "If it's business—" he started to say before she halted him with a slight wave of one hand.

"I wish it were as straightforward as something to do with business," she told him.

"Then what is it?" he asked, deciding to be blunt about it. Maybe it was none of his concern, but now that his curiosity was roused, he couldn't let it go, either. Not unless she kicked him out.

But for once, Amanda Bradley didn't seem capable of doing that, and as if recognizing she was stuck with him, she said, "What I've got on my mind involves four young children." She paused for a beat. "Relatives, actually."

That caught Dev off guard. "Relatives?" he repeated after a moment.

"Yes," she said, again meeting his gaze. "These particular children happen to be my sisters and brothers."

What? He realized his mouth was in danger of falling open. She was an only child who'd moved to Jester with her parents when she was just a slip of a girl. He knew that as well as he knew his own name. Hell, everyone who'd been in town for a while knew it.

"How in the world," he had to ask her, "can you have sisters and brothers?"

"I can if my father had more children after he left Jester. Which, I just recently learned, he did."

Chapter Two

There, it was out, what she'd kept to herself for days.

And having shared it with someone, Amanda had to concede that she felt better. True, she'd never expected to share it with the man who continued to stare down at her. Not any more than she'd expected to find him in her living room. In fact, if anyone had told her that morning that she'd be tending to Dev Devlin's wounds before the day was over, she would have questioned their sanity. Just as he'd looked ready to question hers moments ago.

"Technically," he said as his expression settled into more thoughtful lines, "that means you have some half sisters and brothers."

"Yes," she agreed, "but, to me, it's one and the same. My father also fathered them, and even if I never saw them face-to-face, I'd still feel there's nothing 'half' about our relationship."

"Hmm. I suppose you've got a point." He walked over and eased himself down on the other end of the sofa. "Do you plan on seeing them?"

The answer to that one, Amanda recognized, was far more complicated than a simple "yes," even assuming he'd be satisfied with a single-word reply. She hadn't missed the probing look accompanying his question. Still, she only had to tell him what she wanted to, and logic prompted her to consider the benefits of discussing as much as she felt comfortable doing. After all, she'd already discovered how a small weight could be lifted from her shoulders by sharing some information.

"I do plan on seeing them," she replied at last. "In fact, ever since I learned about them days ago, I've been determined to at least do that much."

"I take it," he said, "that up until then you didn't know about them at all."

"Not until I received a phone call from an attorney who not only told me they existed, but that they were orphans and wards of the state."

It took him less than a minute to absorb that information. "Which means your father is..." His voice trailed off as his expression sobered.

Although Amanda's throat tightened, she was determined not to shed any more tears. "Yes, I was told that he passed away a year ago in Minnesota."

"I'm sorry." The words were simply spoken but seemed completely genuine.

"Thank you," she said.

And that was all she would say on the subject of her father's death, the details of which she had no intention of discussing with him, or anyone else in Jester. The town's longtime residents already had memories of Sherman Bradley, and one of them was hardly flattering. They didn't need to know everything.

As if he had no trouble recalling that less-than-flattering episode in her family's history, Dev said, "So after your father, ah, left Jester, he went to Minnesota?"

"You mean after he ran off with Rita Winslow, his attractive young co-worker at the savings and loan," she corrected, deciding to be candid about what they both knew was the blunt truth of the matter. "Yes, they apparently chose to put some distance between themselves and this town." In the process, they'd left her and probably most everyone in Jester in a state of shock, Amanda remembered. Up until a few days after her fifteenth birthday, her always dapperly dressed father had been a well-respected accountant, one many considered the image of the ideal family man. Then, just like that, he was gone.

In the months that followed, her mother had filed for a divorce on the grounds of desertion, and five years later Mary Bradley had quietly passed away after a short illness with only her daughter, who'd made a hasty trip back from college, at her side.

"Eventually," Amanda said, forging on with her story, "my father and Rita Winslow were married, and years later when she found herself a widow, Rita returned to Pine Run, where she was born and raised, even though she had no family left in the area." Just twenty miles away, Amanda reflected, but she'd had no idea that the larger town southwest of Jester had once again become home to her father's second wife.

"With Rita," she continued, "came the children she and my father had brought into the world. A girl who's now seven years old, two boys now five and four, and another girl, only a baby really, who's eighteen months old."

Dev stretched out his long legs and stacked one booted foot over the other. "Sounds as though they waited a while to have kids."

Amanda nodded, acknowledging the truth of that.

After all, fifteen years had passed since Sherman Bradley had disappeared in the middle of the night with his suitcases packed and a brief note left behind to say he wasn't coming back.

"And then," she said, "they had four children in fairly rapid succession."

"Children you referred to earlier as orphans," he reminded her, "which has to mean that their mother is gone, too."

"I'm afraid so." She released a quiet breath. "After Rita returned to Pine Run, she took a job in a local lawyer's office. When that same lawyer phoned to tell me about my father and the children, he also said that Rita had been killed in an automobile accident over a month ago. As her employer, he'd volunteered to go through her papers to help settle her estate, and that was when he discovered a copy of my parents' final divorce decree, which my father must have obtained at some point from the district court. Along with it were some small school photos of me he'd apparently taken with him. They were bound together with an old newspaper article in the *Pine Run Plain Talker* mentioning that Amanda Bradley, a Jester resident, had been one of the winners in a spelling contest."

"And that's how the lawyer found you." He shook his head. "He'd never have found me if he'd had to rely on my winning any spelling contests."

Which, Dev thought as Amanda only met that rueful remark with silence, had a lot less to do with intelligence than the fact that there had been a time when he'd seldom applied the brains he had. He'd been too busy raising hell on a regular basis. But that had all changed.

"I take it," he said, "that you're going to Pine Run to see the kids."

Her gaze didn't waver. "Yes, but beyond just seeing them, there's a hearing scheduled at the offices of Child and Family Services next Tuesday, and I plan on doing my best to convince the authorities to place the children in my care."

Well, she had guts to even consider taking on that kind of responsibility. He couldn't deny that. "Think you'll be successful?"

Her sudden sigh was long and heartfelt. "I wish I could say so with any certainty, but it may turn out to be an uphill battle if I can't convince the authorities that I have enough resources to make it the most appealing solution."

Resources. At least a part of that, Dev figured, had to translate to money, which he now had the ability to supply with little trouble. Of course, that also applied to several other people who'd shared in the lottery. Then again, even though Amanda could count at least a few of those newly wealthy as her friends, she wouldn't be asking anyone for anything, not unless her back was flat against the wall. He'd be willing to bet on that as a sure thing, because past experience had already gone a long way to show she could be as mule-headed as anybody he'd ever met. If he was right, the last thing she'd do was ask for financial help.

But that wouldn't be necessary in his case. Given that she had something he wanted, they could make a fair trade.

It was so damn simple…if he could talk her into it.

"If finances are a problem," he said, keeping his tone mild, "we can solve it here and now. I'm ready to make you a decent enough offer for the bookstore property that you could open another one somewhere else in town and probably still have a healthy profit left over.''

Her chin went up. An automatic response? Dev wondered. Either that or his reviving a sore subject had teed her off all over again. Noting that the color had returned to her face, he wouldn't have been surprised to see her stalk over the door, wrench it open and firmly suggest he waste no time in leaving. But she didn't.

All at once it seemed far too quiet as seconds ticked by. At last, Amanda broke the silence. ''I'll…think about letting you make me that offer.''

Dev resisted the urge to heave a gusty sigh. Maybe, just maybe, he told himself, he would finally be able to put an end, once and for all, to the continual friction between them. ''All right,'' he said in the most businesslike tone he could muster, ''you can let me know what you decide.''

With that, he got up. ''I'll take off now.'' He strode to the chair, retrieved his hat and settled it on his head.

Amanda stood as he pulled on his jacket. ''I probably won't have an answer for you until after the hearing on Tuesday. And I'm not,'' she added candidly, ''at all sure what it will be.''

If she was telling him not to get his hopes up, Dev knew it was too late. Not that he considered the whole thing anywhere near a done deal, but she'd agreed to think about it, and right now he was counting himself lucky for that much.

''I'll drop by the bookstore after you get back from Pine Run,'' he told her.

She arched a wry eyebrow. ''Well, that will be a

definite switch. You haven't exactly been one of my best customers."

"You haven't been one of mine, either," he reminded her with a wry look of his own as he started to turn toward the door. Then his denim-clad thigh brushed against an edge of the shoulder bag resting on the end table and toppled it over. He dropped down to grab it before it hit the floor.

"I'll take it," Amanda said, stepping forward.

He straightened and absently handed the bag over, his attention already captured by the book that had been exposed, one featuring a bold cover he now had no trouble making out. "*Midnight Passions*," he murmured, reading the title. He glanced at Amanda. "I usually favor the newspaper when it comes to keeping up on things, but I've got to admit that your choice in reading material seems...interesting."

Ignoring that dry comment, she tossed her purse on the chair and stepped past him to head for the door. Although she didn't wrench it open, she didn't linger over it, either.

"Good night," she told him, oh-so-politely.

"Good night," he replied, matching her tone. "Happy reading," he added as he walked out, tossing that short statement over his shoulder. The only reply he got was the sound of the door snapping shut. Dev had to grin. Even if it made his cut lip burn like a son of a gun, it was worth it.

He'd finally had the last word with Amanda Bradley.

THE DRIVE TO Pine Run gave Amanda more than enough time to think about several things. Nevertheless, again and again, her thoughts drifted back to Dev

Devlin. Could she really sell her share of the building to him? Could she give in at last?

A firm answer to that question continued to elude her as she followed a curve in the two-lane highway cutting a path through the rolling hills that flowed like gentle waves over the eastern part of Montana. She remembered her first sight of the area when she was eight years old and a new arrival from the far flatter plains of the central Midwest. To her, the hills had been mountains, and the town of Jester, with its long Western history, almost a small piece of another world.

Soon after she and her parents had moved into the house Amanda now owned, they'd walked over to Main Street to see the place where her father would be starting his new job. Back then, she hadn't so much as considered the possibility that she would one day open a bookstore only steps from the old brick building that was home to Jester Savings and Loan.

That was the same sunny summer day she'd seen Dev Devlin for the very first time, she couldn't help but recall, and even to her pre-adolescent eyes, he'd been a memorable sight when she'd passed him on the sidewalk just doors down from the Heartbreaker Saloon. She'd never expected him, or any teenage boy, to notice her.

Yet he had, giving her a slow smile as their eyes met for a brief moment—a smile she'd done her best to return in her own shy fashion. Then he'd continued on his way, swaggering just a bit in his threadbare T-shirt and battered jeans, and she'd thought that maybe she'd made an acquaintance in town, if not a real friend.

But that was before her young ears had picked up

on some pointed comments about the local "bad boy."

"That Devlin kid," a longtime Jester resident had contended within Amanda's hearing, "is primed to go down the same road as the rest of his shiftless family."

"Any girl who gets involved with him is just plain looking for trouble," someone else had said.

Having spent most of her brief life being a "good girl" in an effort to please the father she adored, Amanda had taken those comments to heart and given the bad boy a wide berth. Only after she'd returned to Jester as a full-grown woman had she felt ready to take on the man Dev Devlin had become.

The undeniable truth that she'd done it, had taken on both him and his rowdy saloon, made it ever harder to consider selling out to him now. Could she really give in? Amanda wondered yet again.

Yes, she finally decided, releasing a long breath. She not only could do it, she would do it…if the fate of four children depended on it.

Which it just might, Amanda told herself as she swung her gray compact into the parking lot of the brown brick building housing the local division of Child and Family Services. She'd know soon enough what had to be done, she more than suspected. The fact that she still hadn't shared the news about her sisters and brothers with anyone besides Dev Devlin by no means meant that she'd considered for even one minute backing off on her plan to do everything possible to further her chances of being allowed to provide a home for her newfound relatives.

With that goal still firmly in mind, she straightened the fitted jacket of her cream-colored wool suit and tried to look every inch the competent and responsible woman as she entered a small reception area. There, she met the Pine Run attorney who had stunned her down to her toes when he'd phoned her after being somewhat surprised himself to learn that she existed.

"Pleased to meet you, my dear," Clarence Whipple told her in the courtly fashion of a silver-haired man probably close to seventy. Short of stature and built along thin lines, he wore a three-piece, pin-striped suit with comfortable ease, as though he'd been born into the legal profession. "I know this must be a very important day for you."

"It is," Amanda agreed as they shook hands.

Clarence pulled a small envelope from his well-worn briefcase. "I have the school photos and newspaper article that initially led me to you. I thought you would like to have them." He gave the sealed envelope to Amanda. "I also took the liberty of including a recent snapshot of your half siblings, one of several I came across."

She put the envelope in her shoulder bag. "That was very kind of you. I know I must have sounded astonished when you first called me."

"Yes, you could say that," he murmured with a trace of wry humor before his expression settled into more serious lines. "I was pleased to be able to tell you about the children, even though I also had the regrettable task of conveying the information that your father had passed away—and under somewhat, er, unfortunate circumstances."

Yes, those circumstances had definitely been unfortunate, Amanda thought. She had to appreciate Clarence Whipple's tact in giving the matter no more than a mere mention now. "How difficult do you think it will be for me to get custody?"

The lawyer met her gaze. "I can only say that, on one hand, your being the closest relative still living will work in your favor. On the other hand, a drawback is the fact that you're single, and placement with a married couple is usually preferred. I believe the outcome will depend on whether we can convince the authorities that putting the children in your care is the most satisfactory solution for them."

Amanda nodded. "Before things get started, can you tell me more about what their mother was like?" It was something she'd found herself wondering about more than once during the last several days, since she only had the barest memories of the woman who had become her father's second wife. A tall, full-figured blonde with a ready smile for visitors to Jester Savings and Loan was how Amanda remembered Rita Winslow.

"She applied for a position in my office soon after returning to Montana," Clarence said. "My first impression was that Rita had changed from the young, and I suppose I have to say somewhat flighty, woman I recalled from her earlier days in Pine Run. Rather than skirting the issue, as some might have been inclined to do, she was forthright about the details of her life in Minnesota and how she'd become a widow there. When she went on to candidly admit that she needed a job to support her children, I decided to take her on for a probationary period to see how things went. As it happened, she turned out to be a good worker, and I came to like her more than enough to be both shocked and saddened by the accident that took her life."

"Thank goodness the children weren't with her in the car," Amanda had to say, having already learned during the initial phone conversation with the lawyer that Rita had been on her way to pick them up at a baby-sitter's house after work when she'd apparently hit an icy patch in the road.

"Mr. McFadden is ready to see you now," the young brunette acting as receptionist told them. "His office is just down the hall, first door on the right."

They followed directions, and in a matter of seconds Amanda met Haynes McFadden, supervisor of the local division. The long and lean man with a balding head rimmed by sandy hair in turn introduced a middle-aged woman occupying one of the visitor's chairs set in front of a modern oak desk. "This is Louise Pearson, one of our longtime and most dedicated employees. Mrs. Pearson is currently handling the Bradley case."

That name got Amanda's attention in a hurry. Although they'd never met face-to-face before, she knew that Louise Pearson was no stranger to Jester. In fact, she'd been the social worker involved in the case of a baby left in the Brimming Cup coffee shop shortly after Amanda's good friend Shelly Dupree—now Shelly O'Rourke with her recent marriage—had become one of the big jackpot winners. Although the episode had ended happily with the mother's eventual return to claim her child, Amanda had no trouble recalling how Louise had been described as a person to be reckoned with.

As if to prove it, the woman with dark brown hair well-threaded with gray and pulled back in a neat bun, rose to her feet and squared sturdily built shoulders covered by a plain navy suit. Her sharp hazel eyes met Amanda's gaze head-on.

"I have the children waiting to meet you in another

room,'' Louise said, her tone brisk. ''I've already explained the relationship to them, but I'm sure they still have questions. It might be better if you took a few minutes to get acquainted before we come back here for a more private discussion of the details of your situation.''

Well, this was it, Amanda thought. She drew in a steadying breath. ''All right.''

''I'll wait for you here,'' Clarence told her as he lowered himself into a visitor's chair. Again he was being tactful, and Amanda had to be grateful one more time. It would be hard enough, she suspected, to keep her composure without an audience around.

At a gestured invitation, Amanda followed Louise across the room toward a side door. The older woman paused with one hand on the knob and glanced back at Amanda. ''Before we go in, I think it would be wise to get something straight. The bottom line with me is that I want what's best for these children.''

Recognizing the truth underscoring that straightforward statement, Amanda replied, ''So do I.''

Louise studied her for a moment. ''I'm glad to find we agree on that.'' And with those words, she opened the door.

Stepping through it, Amanda found herself in a narrow conference room. At its center stood an oval-shaped oak table currently covered with a variety of coloring books and crayons, and seated around it were the children who had already made a permanent place for themselves in Amanda's mind.

Now, watching as four pairs of brown eyes stared back at her—eyes so much like her father's…and like her own—Amanda felt the impact of that sight hit her straight in the heart. Her sisters and brothers, she thought. On the day each was born, they had become a part of her, and she a part of them.

"Hello," she said, summoning the brightest smile she could.

It won her a smile in turn from the smallest person in the room, a little charmer with a chubby-cheeked face framed by tiny golden curls. In contrast, the other children, all with hair as short, blond and curly as their youngest sibling, merely continued to stare.

Louise formally introduced them, although Amanda already knew the basics regarding their names and ages. Seven-year-old Liza was the eldest. Like her younger brothers, Caleb and Patrick, she was as slender as a reed. Only eighteen-month-old Betsy was more round than slim. All were dressed in a colorful mix of well-worn cotton pants and long-sleeved T-shirts.

Amanda pulled out a padded oak chair and took a seat next to Liza, who held Betsy in her lap. "I'm so happy to meet you." She let her gaze connect with each of the children as she looked around the table. "I'm Amanda, your—" she had to swallow against a sudden tightness before she got it out "—big sister."

"Amadaba," Betsy said, offering another smile.

"I guess it is quite a mouthful," Amanda admitted with a slight curve of her lips. "How about if you all call me Mandy?" No one except her parents had ever used that name, but at the moment it seemed undeniably right.

"Mandeee!" Betsy declared, clapping her tiny hands.

"Yes, you've got it," Amanda told the pint-size girl.

"She's very smart," Liza offered in a small voice that nonetheless held more than a hint of pride.

Amanda nodded. "I don't doubt that for a minute. In fact, I wouldn't be a bit amazed if you're all smart."

"Why?" That question came from five-year-old Caleb, who sat across the table.

"Because our father was a very smart man." Which was no more than pure fact, Amanda reflected with assurance. It would have been surprising if anyone had ever contended that Sherman Bradley was less than intelligent. No, whatever his weaknesses had been, they couldn't be blamed on any lack of brainpower.

"So we got the same daddy," Patrick, the youngest boy at four, summed up with a solemn look. "And now he's in heaven, with my mommy."

Tears pricked at Amanda's eyes, but she refused to give in to them. These children, she told herself, didn't need any more tears in their lives. What they needed was someone to love them.

And she did. There was simply no question about that. The sheer truth was that she'd fallen head over heels at her very first sight of them. "I know you've all been through a bad time, but there are better things ahead."

"Like what?" Caleb wanted to know, a small glint of what might have been hope gleaming in his gaze.

Amanda knew she had to pick her words carefully. She couldn't tell them they would have a home with her. Not yet. "Well, for one thing, you get to live in Montana." It was as enthusiastic a statement as she could make it. "You know, not too far west of where we are now there are mountains so tall they almost seem to touch the sky, and rivers that run so fast the fish don't even have to swim—the water just pushes them along."

Both boys smiled at that while Betsy clapped again. Only Liza continued to fix Amanda with a wary stare.

"Do cowboys live there?" Caleb asked, seeming to be the most curious of the group.

"Not only there, but all over this state," Amanda told him. "They wear wide-brimmed hats with straight-legged jeans and shirts with shiny snaps down the front." *All of which described the Western-style clothing the Heartbreaker Saloon's owner favored.*

Abruptly an image formed in Amanda's mind, one she ousted in the next breath. She didn't want to think about Dev Devlin and the fact that he'd probably waste little time in tracking her down when she returned to Jester. He'd no doubt be champing at the bit to learn if she was going to let him make her an offer for her property. And she was, she knew, if it would mean keeping these children out of a foster home run by strangers.

"I wanna be a cowboy," Patrick said, regaining her attention.

"Me be cabboy!" Betsy tossed in.

Amanda had to laugh. "Well, I don't see why you can't all be cowboys—and cowgirls." She looked at Liza. "Would you like to be high on a horse's back riding herd on a bunch of cattle?"

The girl shook her head, her expression still sober. "That's just make-believe."

"Not necessarily," Louise countered in a soft tone, entering the conversation from where she stood near the door. The social worker didn't look quite as formidable when she spoke to the eldest Bradley child. "Sometimes make-believe can come true."

Although Liza said nothing in response, she looked far from ready to agree with that concept.

Louise redirected her gaze toward Amanda, and once again her voice turned brisk. "I think it's time to let the children color some more pictures while we talk."

No, it's too soon for me to leave them, Amanda wanted to say. And didn't. Rising, she again smiled down at her newfound relatives. "Goodbye for now," she said.

"Bye-bye," Betsy offered with a little wave.

Amanda's smiled slipped as she struggled for her composure. Then she waved in return and headed for the door Louise held open for her. All she could think was that, no matter what it took, she had to convince the authorities that she was the right choice to care for four orphaned children. Somehow, she had to do that.

She had to.

DEV FIGURED he was pushing things when he walked into Ex-Libris the following morning, but the plain truth was that he'd had a hard time telling himself to wait at least a couple of days after Amanda returned from Pine Run before he learned how she'd made out. After their earlier conversation, he was just too optimistic to hold back.

With any luck, he thought, she'd tell him that her plan to gain custody was proceeding smoothly enough that all she needed was a hefty contribution to her bank account to seal the deal. Yeah, if good fortune was on his side, it wouldn't be long until he'd be expanding his business while she relocated hers, and everyone would come out a winner.

Dev glanced around him, not much surprised to find

the bookstore empty. It was still early, at least by Main Street standards. More than a few storeowners would just be starting their day. The Ex-Libris's owner had to be around somewhere, though, he reflected as he walked toward a small sitting area at the rear of the store. And, sure enough, that's where he found her, seated on one of a pair of burgundy leather love seats. Today she wore another of her tailored blouses with pleated wool trousers and was gazing down at something she held in one hand. As far as he could make out, it was a small photograph.

"Good morning," he said as he came to a halt inches from a low, bowlegged mahogany table covered with a lacey white cloth. It wasn't yet loaded with the homemade pastries Gwen Tanner would probably be delivering soon. Gwen was another Big Draw lottery winner and no longer needed to sell her baked goods to supplement the income coming in from her boarding house, but he'd heard that she continued to supply the bookstore, anyway.

Certainly Amanda Bradley looked as though she could use something to tempt her appetite and maybe perk her up a bit. No, a lot, Dev amended on closer inspection. For the second time in less than a week, she seemed to bear little resemblance to the stubborn female who'd regularly raked him over the coals.

"Good morning," she replied, finally returning his greeting as she glanced up at him. She set the snapshot she'd been holding down on the table.

Dev got a better gander at it as he eased himself into one of the twin burgundy chairs that matched the love seats. Four curly-haired, towheaded kids grinned at the camera in a scene that featured a small Christmas tree in the background along with a few presents that looked freshly unwrapped. Apparently the kids hadn't gotten a lot from Santa on that particular Christmas morning, but they looked happy enough with what they had. One thing for sure, their expressions were a lot more enthusiastic than Amanda's.

"Things didn't go well in Pine Run," he said, deciding to cut to the chase as he stacked an ankle on a denim-clad knee and reached up to thumb back his Stetson.

"No." She let out a thin sigh. "I tried everything I could think of to make them see the advantages of placing the children with me, but…"

"But they didn't go for it," he finished when her voice drifted off.

"And I don't for the life of me know what I could have done differently." All at once she raised a small fist and slapped it down on a plump cushion, displaying a hint of the temper he was more familiar with. "Oh, they were impressed that I owned a home, free and clear. They also appreciated the fact that I had a buyer not only ready but eager to purchase another piece of property, which would increase my immediate income." The last came out with a wry twist of her lips and a meaningful look aimed his way. "But in the end they felt my sisters and brothers needed, and I quote, 'a more stable environment than a single caretaker could provide.'"

"That's a tough one," he said, keeping his voice low.

"And then—" She leaned her head against the back of the love seat and studied the high ceiling. "And then they went on to say that the children would be placed into permanent foster care. All except the youngest, they told me oh-so-reasonably. Betsy's only eighteen months old, so she would mostly likely be put up for adoption.''

''Jeez,'' Dev muttered under his breath, watching as Amanda let out another, almost soundless, sigh.

''I can't believe they'll be separated.'' How she felt on that score was as plain as the grim bleakness in her tone. ''I'd give anything—do *anything*—to be able to change what's about to happen to them.''

But what the hell more could she give? Dev asked himself, his own temper flaring at what seemed liked the injustice of it all. What did a bunch of bureaucrats expect her to do? As far as they were apparently concerned, a ''single caretaker''—even one who owned a home and had a golden opportunity to add to her bank account—just didn't fill the bill, and that was it.

So, being undeniably single, what was Amanda Bradley supposed to do? It was a devil of a problem, all right. And even with his money, he couldn't help her solve it.

That's not quite true, Devlin, something inside him said. *There's one thing you could do, but it would have to go a long way beyond getting out your checkbook.*

Jolted by that thought, he made a stab at ignoring the voice rumbling in the back of his mind, only to find that he couldn't block it out. Not any more than he could stop his gaze from again being drawn to the happy faces of four grinning kids—kids who just might be looking a long way from cheerful at the moment. He knew he'd have been a lot more successful in resisting the sight of those rosy-cheeked faces in his younger, wilder days. Back then, he'd had little trouble avoiding anything that didn't involve his own immediate health and welfare.

But you changed when you decided to show Jester's

residents a thing or two by becoming a person they could respect, the niggling voice contended.

Dev drew in a long breath, admitting the truth of that. Even though he'd never had any desire to get tied up in town politics, these days he was by and large an upstanding citizen. But that didn't mean the slate was wiped clean. Maybe he still had some private dues to pay for all the years when he mostly hadn't given a damn about anyone except himself.

The man he'd once been would have scoffed at that notion. The man he'd become flat-out couldn't.

Trouble was, Dev thought as he slowly lifted his gaze, the woman seated across from him might not hesitate to scoff. "In fact, she just might think I'm crazy if I even mention what I'm considering," he muttered under his breath.

But the idea had taken hold, he couldn't deny. Somehow, now that he'd latched on to it, it seemed pretty much the only thing to do. Which didn't mean that he'd have a lot of choice except to let the whole business go if she *did* tell him he was crazy.

He just hoped to hell she didn't laugh at him, because if she did, he was sure to start growling at her again and the truce they'd somehow managed to maintain for weeks would be history.

"It seems to me there might be a way to persuade the authorities to change their mind," he said, picking his words carefully.

In response, Amanda continued to stare up at the ceiling. "I've been racking my brain ever since I left Family Services trying to come up with something. To me, it appears pretty hopeless, but if you've got a suggestion, I'm willing to hear it."

He ran his tongue around his teeth, then just plunged in. "You could get married."

That got her attention in a hurry. She abandoned the ceiling to stare at him. "I know we haven't exactly been friendly since I came back to Jester and opened up my store, but most people here could probably pass along the news that I haven't even been dating anyone lately. Believe me, there's no husband on the horizon."

"That could change," he told her.

"Not anytime soon," she countered.

"It could...if you married me."

Chapter Three

Amanda's eyes went wide. She couldn't have been more astounded if Dev Devlin had just suggested that she strip down to her underwear and do a wild dance on top of the bar at the Heartbreaker Saloon.

"You have got to be kidding," she told him in no uncertain terms.

"I'm not," he assured her in the same candid tone. "Since you're looking at me like I've gone right around the bend, though, I guess I should add that the marriage wouldn't have to last all that long. Once we get through the adoption process and you have legal custody, there's no reason the whole thing can't be quietly dissolved at some point in the future."

But she was still caught up in the here and now. "The two of us...married?" She couldn't even imagine it.

"Boggles the mind, I agree," he said dryly, looking her straight in the eye.

Amanda frowned as her brain finally started to function. "Why in the world would you so much as think of doing this?"

He shrugged a broad shoulder. "Could be getting a

glimpse of those kids—'' he dipped his head toward the photo on the table ''—got to me.''

She had to stare at him. ''I never expected you to be the sentimental type.''

''Me, either,'' he confessed, just gruffly enough to have her suspecting that he'd been at least a bit surprised himself by the offer that had stunned her down to the ground.

It was a side of him she hadn't seen before and made her wonder what else she didn't know about Dev Devlin. Judging by his undeniable success even before he'd hit it big in the lottery, the former bad boy had become a shrewd businessman. Nevertheless, he was still far from a likely candidate for a married lifestyle. She simply couldn't believe otherwise. ''You can't be trying to tell me you want to be a husband.''

He blew out what might have been an exasperated breath. ''I'm telling you that I'd go along with it if it will keep four young kids from who knows what kind of future. I know we've been a long way from chummy in the past, but even you and I can agree on that score.''

Amanda didn't have to have twenty-twenty vision to see the truth of his words reflected in the deep blue eyes that were all but drilling themselves into hers. He really was thinking of the children. And, as amazing as it seemed, she had to concede that his suggestion just might merit some consideration.

Desperation, she thought. That had to be it.

''There's no guarantee, you know, that I'll be allowed to adopt them even if I do get married,'' she pointed out as the most practical part of her began to examine the situation.

He folded his arms across the wide chest covered

by his short leather jacket. "Since you'll be marrying a millionaire, they aren't likely to quibble about the financial aspects, at any rate."

Her chin went up in a flash. "I don't want your money."

A smile played around the corners of his mouth. "Believe me, I know that doesn't even enter into it, not as far as you're concerned."

Her pride soothed, she said, "Good." Then it occurred to her that walking down the aisle was normally expected to lead to sharing far more than a bank account.

"It would, of course," she added very deliberately, "be a marriage in name only."

His smile only widened in a way that, for some reason, put everything female inside her on full alert.

"No sex," he murmured in a suddenly lazy drawl.

"None," she shot back, telling herself that her pulse had only picked up several beats in delayed reaction to his startling proposal. Physical awareness had nothing to do with it. In fact, nothing physical—or emotional, for that matter—would have to be involved in a marriage in name only.

His gaze didn't waver for a moment. "Well, the new house I plan on moving into this weekend has enough bedrooms that four kids plus two adults will fill them up nicely."

"If we decide to go through with it," she tacked on, far from ready to come to any conclusions.

He nodded. "It's your call. If you say the word, it shouldn't take more than a few days to set things up. We can get a judge to marry us at the courthouse in Pine Run and head over to Family Services the minute it's done."

And could the marriage be annulled if they failed to get the authorities to change their mind? Probably, Amanda reflected, though she was beginning to doubt that question would even arise. Something told her that Dev Devlin could be persuasive when he wanted to, even if he hadn't managed to bring her around to his way of thinking after months of trying to buy her out. She'd dug in her heels because her emotions were involved, and monetary gain had come a distant second.

If one looked at the custody situation logically, however, as the authorities were bound to do, placing her sisters and brothers in the care of a married couple whose financial circumstances couldn't be faulted had to be considered an advantage as far as the children were concerned. And the fact that one half of that couple was a close—and undeniably caring—relative could surely only be viewed, even by the sharp eyes of most dedicated of government employees, as another plus.

But would they question the fact that the caring relative and her new husband cared about each other?

Amanda watched her companion brush a stray strand of hair off his forehead. Once that thick, wheat-colored hair had nearly reached his shoulders, she remembered. Now it was cut short enough to be judged conservative. "Have you considered the fact that, even if we went through with it, we may well have to convince Family Services that our marriage is a love match?"

He mulled that over for a moment. "I'd say we can do it."

"How?" she had to ask.

"I can talk a pretty good tale," he told her. "Believe it or not, some people have even been known to think I have my own brand of charm."

She would have liked to snort at that—might have actually done it if she didn't know that this man was a big hit with more than a few of the ladies in Jester.

"All you have to do is follow my lead," he added, "provided you decide you're willing to go through with this."

Was she willing? That, Amanda knew, was the real question. Certainly she'd never planned on becoming a bride strictly out of necessity, and she was by no means sure how many of her feelings she could put on hold. Even if this was a marriage in name only, with no physical or emotional commitment, could she enter into it as a purely practical means to achieve a goal and see it end without regrets?

Because it *would* end, eventually. The nature of their relationship up until this point and the fact that they were basically so different was enough to have her certain that she and Dev Devlin would go their separate ways.

But not before they had the opportunity to do their best to ensure the safety of four young orphans. And that was the bottom line, she realized. Hadn't she said she would give anything—do *anything*—to change their fate? Now she'd been given the power to at least make a real attempt to keep them together as a family. Her family. All she had to do was say…

"Yes."

Amanda got the word out, maintaining a steady gaze on someone she'd never by any stretch of the imagination considered husband material. "Yes, I'm willing to go through with it."

AT LEAST she hadn't laughed at him. Dev figured his ego would have to be content with that, because it hadn't escaped his notice that Amanda had hardly been eager to accept his offer yesterday. It was his fault for going off half-cocked and offering in the first place, he supposed.

Not that he was sorry he'd done it. Not when you considered the fact that he'd had no trouble sleeping last night, and if he'd turned his back on those tow-headed kids, they'd probably have haunted his dreams. So he wasn't sorry, and the best thing to do now was make sure things went off without a hitch.

"What's new in the world?" Roy Gibson asked as he stacked clean glasses behind the massive oak bar that stretched nearly the length of the saloon.

Dev glanced up from the Billings newspaper he hadn't been paying much mind to. His usual routine was to read the *Billings Gazette* from cover to cover, along with the smaller *Pine Run Plain Talker,* and most mornings he had little problem concentrating on the news of the day. Not so today, though.

"Nothing major happening that I've latched on to so far," he replied truthfully enough to the man he'd hired as the Heartbreaker's head bartender once business had begun to pick up and the place had started making a regular profit. Now he'd taken on another bartender, as well, but Roy continued to be in charge whenever the saloon's owner wasn't around.

"I reckon anytime a headline doesn't leap out at you, that's good news," Roy said in the Western twang he'd never lost from his earlier days in Texas. He could pour a draft beer with the precision of a skilled surgeon, although as far as appearances were concerned, he favored the outlaw look of a Willie Nelson—long gray braids and all.

Actually, when it came to news, Dev thought as he shifted on his stool and reached for the thick coffee mug resting next to the spread-out paper, he had some that would probably have jaws dropping all over Jester once it hit. Until the knot was tied, however, he and Amanda had agreed to keep it under wraps.

"While I think about it," he said, "I won't be around next Monday. You and Lonnie will have to handle things between you."

Roy dipped his head in a nod. "No problem. Mondays are usually slow, anyway."

Which was true enough, Dev knew. That's why he'd picked it as his wedding day. As for today, once Irene Caldwell could come in and man the bookstore for a few hours, he and Amanda planned to slip away and make a quick trip to Pine Run to take care of the necessary details, so things would be all set for the ceremony.

He already had a good suit, one he'd had tailor-made for him to celebrate his big win. As to what Amanda would choose to wear for the wedding, he had no idea. It was a pretty good bet, though, that it would be something the fancy magazines called "stylish." Which meant the last thing he wanted to do was look like a small-town hick when they stood together in front of a judge. Maybe he'd never spent much time in a really big city, but he could look as though he belonged in one if he had to.

"You wouldn't be following Dean Kenning's example and sneaking off for a hot date, would you?" The question came right along with an amused glint in Roy's eye.

Dev had to chuckle, low in his throat. More than a few of the town's citizens had often suspected that the bachelor barber had done more than buy lottery tickets for Jester's longtime players when he'd made his weekly trips to Pine Run.

"I'll leave the hot dates to Dean," Dev said, and didn't miss the way Roy's gaze abruptly turned probing.

"Seems to me you haven't been doing any dating lately."

Dev sipped his coffee. "Maybe I'm saving myself for a good woman."

"A *good* woman?" Roy threw his head back and roared. "You're gonna have me splitting my sides if you keep talking like that."

"Don't laugh too hard," Dev advised, deciding it wouldn't hurt to plant a few seeds before the news of the wedding got around. It probably wouldn't do Amanda's chances of getting custody any good if the real reason behind the marriage became general knowledge. "I just might think it's time to change a few of my habits when it comes to the female half of the population," he added.

And maybe he'd already made that decision somewhere along the way, he admitted to himself. The plain truth was that he'd been living like a monk for a while now, and not because he'd lacked opportunities to spend some private time with a woman—including Mary Kay Thompson, a pert, permed blonde with a penchant for wearing tight capri pants and thin tank tops who'd set her beady sights on him after failing to get to first base with Jack Hartman after the local vet had become another of the "Main Street Millionaires," as some people had dubbed the winners.

If he wanted to take a guess as to why the considerable charms of willing women in general, and the all-too-eager Mary Kay in particular, hadn't moved him, Dev supposed he'd have to say that his hormones seemed to be waiting for something else. Something…more. Hell, as far as sheer honesty went, the only woman he'd even thought about so much as kissing lately was—

"Could be you have a point about a few things changing when it comes to females," Roy said, breaking into Dev's thoughts. "Lord knows, I never expected to see the time when you and Amanda Bradley would go weeks without an out-and-out argument."

"I've learned she can be reasonable," Dev replied, keeping his tone casual as he planted more seeds. Not that he believed for a minute that the Ex-Libris's owner couldn't stick to her guns when she wanted to. She'd put her foot down firmly enough when it came to future bedroom activities, and she'd meant it.

No sex. He had to hope he wouldn't wind up cursing the day he'd agreed to that one, because it meant he obviously wouldn't be getting any for some time, from Amanda or anyone else.

Despite having earned the nickname "Devil Devlin," he had his standards. He'd never had anything to do with a married woman, and as a married man, he knew he'd be keeping his vows as long as the marriage lasted. As to how long that would be, he could only wonder. If the look on Amanda's face when she'd accepted his proposal was any indication, she'd want the whole thing over and done with as quickly as possible.

"Well, she may have turned reasonable," Roy remarked, "but she sure doesn't fit in here."

Although the Heartbreaker and its bookstore neighbor stood side by side, Dev knew it would be hard to imagine two places more different. While he'd been considering some additional improvements, the only thing the saloon could currently lay claim to as being anywhere close to fancy was the new ventilation system he'd had installed a few months back to give everyone's lungs a break from any buildup of cigarette smoke. He doubted the need had ever come up in Amanda's establishment.

"No, she doesn't fit in," he said softly.

The thoughtful expression that quiet agreement produced told Dev his calm responses regarding a woman he'd been known in the past to rant and rave about had stirred the older man's curiosity. Roy followed it up by saying, "When you come right down to it, Amanda Bradley is no common-variety female."

Once again, Dev agreed. "I won't argue with you on that score."

As though unable to resist, Roy leaned in and dropped his voice to a confidential level. "I reckon some would say she's a looker, too, in a kind of refined way."

"Hmm," was the most neutral reply Dev could come up with.

"You got some interest there?" Roy asked, apparently opting for a blunter approach.

Dev allowed himself a small smile. "I just might have," he said, and left it at that. He knew it had achieved its purpose when Roy started whistling a classic country favorite he usually wasted no time in requesting when one of the rotating bands in the area played at the Heartbreaker on Friday and Saturday nights. The man from Texas whistled when he was mulling something over.

Deciding that was enough for the moment, Dev went back to his paper.

He read the weather forecast. Sunny skies were predicted for the next few days. The farmers might not be happy, but Dev was glad to see a break in rain clouds. He was about to turn the page to read the sports report when a picture of a ring featured in a downtown Billings jeweler's ad caught his eye.

Not that the ring was flashy, even if the simply cut stone set squarely in its center was touted to be a four-karat white diamond. The setting, according to the information listed, was antique gold, with a row of diamond chips circling the main stone. "The perfect choice for a real lady," the ad declared in tasteful script letters.

And by God if it wasn't, Dev thought. He'd already planned on picking up a pair of plain gold wedding bands in Pine Run, but this could serve as an engagement ring. Which wasn't strictly necessary, he knew. After all, this particular engagement would only last a matter of days. Still, something was telling him to put that ring on Amanda's finger. Maybe his ego, he admitted. Or more likely his pride.

There was no getting around the fact that his future bride was better educated than he was, given that he'd only made it through high school. Most of Jester's residents would probably say she had better manners, too, at least when she wasn't tearing into him. But, thanks to his newfound wealth, he had something she didn't. He had the means to give her this ring.

And he was damn well going to, he decided. He'd

call the jeweler in Billings and have it express-shipped to him in time for the wedding.

Dev grinned a satisfied grin. He couldn't wait to see his fiancée's reaction when he gave it to her.

"I CAN'T TAKE THIS!" Amanda stared down at the small, velvet-lined box she'd just opened.

"Are you trying to tell me my taste in jewelry is lousy?" Dev asked mildly from the driver's seat of his late-model, saucy-red Jeep that came complete with all the bells and whistles.

She slid him a sidelong glance. "No, of course not. It's…beautiful." Which it was, she thought, again dropping her gaze to a ring that had a stone more than large enough to win notice yet somehow managed to be quietly dignified at the same time. The sun slanting through the windshield glinted off the oval-shaped center diamond, making it sparkle with elegant warmth. Yes, it was beautiful.

"But I don't need it," she added with another look his way.

He twisted the steering wheel to follow a curve in the road. "I know you don't necessarily *need* it. I just wanted you to have it. It's as simple as that."

But it wasn't simple. Not to Amanda. She'd told him she didn't want his money, and that included what was, to her, a far too expensive engagement present. "Can you return it?"

He turned his head to fix his gaze on her for an instant. "I suppose I can, but I'm not going to." More than a hint of firm intent underscored that statement. "Put it on and let's see if it fits."

She shouldn't, she knew. But before she could close the box, the ring winked up at her, and the urge to try it on—just briefly, she told herself—was irresistible. It was the second urge to win out that morning, since she hadn't been able to resist ogling Dev Devlin when he'd arrived on her doorstep. Whatever she'd expected, it wasn't to see him wearing a midnight-blue wool suit that had plainly been the work of an expert tailor. Even though cut along Western lines, it lacked nothing in sophistication. She could only be glad that she'd chosen a slim dress and matching jacket made of ivory silk for her wedding day. Otherwise, she might have felt underdressed in contrast.

Amanda slid the ring on the appropriate finger. "It fits," she said, this time managing to foil the urge to sigh at how right it looked, as though it not only fit her finger, but her.

"I asked the jeweler to size it for a small hand," Dev told her. "I guess I lucked out. Now just keep it on," he added.

"No, it's too—"

He cut her off. "It seems to me we need to start compromising. How about if I get my way on this one and you get yours the next time we butt heads."

"Hmm." Amanda thought about that. "It would almost be worth it to watch you surrender without a battle."

A smile ghosted around his mouth. "Next one goes to you. You've got my word on it—if you keep the ring."

"All right," she said at last. "But don't think I'll forget your promise."

His smile took a wry slant. "Believe me. I'd never expect it to slip your mind."

Amanda decided to quit while she was ahead and try to relax for the rest of the drive. As she leaned back in her seat, she found herself wondering how much her life would change. If things went well at Family Services that afternoon, she would be taking on the responsibility for four young lives. Although a part of her couldn't wait, another part had to question if she'd be up to the task. Well, she would just have to be, she concluded as scattered groups of tall trees just beginning their journey to full spring bloom flashed by.

Her companion drove faster than she usually did, but skillfully, she had to concede. His large hands looked strong and sure on the wheel; his black boots held the gleam of new leather as he pressed down on the accelerator for a fresh burst of speed. All he needed was a Stetson in dress black to complete the picture—and she'd already spied one resting on the back seat.

"How do you want to handle telling the folks back in Jester about the marriage?" he asked.

The sigh she'd held back earlier slipped out. "I'd prefer to do it as quietly as possible—but I don't imagine that's an option."

Dev blew out a gusty breath. "It's bound to be major news," he agreed.

"I already caught Irene looking at me as if she were wondering what I might be up to when I asked her to watch the store again today. If she didn't always seem so happy to do it, I'd feel as though I was imposing on her."

"Now that she's a widow and living at the boarding house, she's probably got time on her hands. I'd say you were doing her a favor." He paused. "Maybe you'd be doing her an even bigger favor if you let her be the one to spread the word about why we're both gone for the day.''

She sat up straight. "Good Lord, I never thought of handling it that way." By rights, Shelly, who'd been a close friend almost since Amanda had first arrived in Jester, should be the first to be told. But Shelly O'Rourke and her doctor husband, Connor, weren't due back from a medical convention in California for another few days. And the woman manning the Ex-Libris at this very moment seemed perfect for the job, Amanda couldn't deny. "Irene would probably be tickled pink to pass along the news, especially since she's been touting the joys of married life to me for a while now."

"Then call her from Pine Run this afternoon, and maybe at least the first round of jaw-dropping will be over by the time we get back tonight."

Tonight. The word reminded Amanda that they still hadn't discussed what would happen on their return. There was no getting around the fact that they had to live together, but... "Are you, ah, ready for me to move into your house?"

That question had him tearing his eyes from the road for another brief glance. "The furniture I've had delivered so far includes two beds, so I guess we're all set."

She nodded with all the briskness she could muster. "Then I'll just pack a bag when we get back and move the rest of my personal belongings later." She might be putting her small home up for rent, as she had when she'd been living in Seattle. At least it was something to consider. Right now, all she knew for sure was that she was in no hurry to return to Jester. As far as she was concerned, long after sundown would be best, when many of the town's ever-curious residents would be in for the night.

"Maybe we could have dinner in Pine Run," she suggested.

Dev mulled that over. "I vote for barbecue."

She rolled her eyes. The man probably ate that kind of food all the time. "I've heard there's a seafood place we could try."

He slowed their speed when traffic started to pick as buildings bordering the outskirts of Pine Run came into view. "Barbecue sounds better to me."

Deciding it wasn't worth the effort, Amanda was about to give in when she remembered their earlier agreement. "You said the next call would be mine," she reminded him, "and I'm coming down on the side of seafood."

"Okay, you win," he said. Then he grinned. "But that means I get my way next time."

Amanda frowned, knowing that she and the man she was about to marry seemed to be such complete opposites that there was sure to be a next time.

Roy Gibson, being a fan of old-time Westerns, would have liked Judge Corbett. Dev had come to that conclusion the minute he first laid eyes on the official who'd agreed to perform the wedding ceremony. With his straightforward stare and a jaw that still seemed rock-solid firm for someone probably in his fifties, the judge might have looked right at home sentencing a frontier gunslinger to swing from the highest tree. That image only faded when the man with jet black hair streaked with silver at the temples smiled and winked an eye nearly as dark as his well-worn robe, which he did now, gazing down at Amanda.

"Well, are you ready to 'get hitched,' as another servant of the court who also happened to be my granddaddy used to say, little lady?"

Standing before an old, heavily carved desk in the judge's chambers, she slid a sidelong look Dev's way. "As ready as I'll ever be, I expect."

The judge followed her glance. "How about you, young man?"

He nodded and fought down a sudden urge to loosen the only silk tie he owned. "Ready, willing and able."

"Then I'll just call in two witnesses and we'll be all set." The judge walked out a side door, leaving his visitors alone for a moment.

"Well, I guess this is it," Dev said. "How are your nerves doing?" He had to admit, at least to himself, that his own could probably have used a medicinal dose of something stronger than the two cups of coffee he'd had at breakfast. Or maybe he shouldn't have had the coffee. Trouble was, he couldn't imagine starting a day without caffeine.

"I promise not to swoon on you," she told him, squaring her shoulders.

That made him chuckle, and he couldn't deny it felt good. "I'd catch you before you hit the carpet," he assured her dryly.

"Thanks," she said, matching his tone.

He aimed a glance around the small room. Functional was about the best he could say for it, although his head bartender would have probably appreciated the faded print of buffalo roaming an open range hung on a narrow strip of beige wall between two tall, bare windows. "Not the most romantic of places, is it?"

She shook her head. "But romance isn't what brought us here."

While he knew she had a point, he also knew women well enough to recognize that sometimes things a man never paid much attention to were important to them. Things like mounds of flowers and a big wedding cake and a bunch of guests to watch the bride walk down the aisle. "I guess it's not exactly the way you imagined you'd get married."

Her quiet sigh was so low he almost missed it. Yeah, she wanted those things, he thought, yet she was ready to do without them for the sake of four kids.

Damn, but he had to admire that. And he'd do everything in his power to make sure she got custody of those kids, too, he vowed. He was going to sweet-talk up a storm when they got to Family Services. If they wanted to see a *love match,* well, they'd see one.

The judge returned with a middle-aged man and younger woman in tow. Dev barely caught their names as they were introduced. Two employees of the court system, he figured. Neither looked particularly enthusiastic at the prospect of witnessing a wedding, but then they were probably used to it.

Judge Corbett cleared his throat. "Let's get started."

And with that, he began the ceremony as Dev and Amanda joined hands. Her skin was cool against his warmth, her smooth palm small enough to get swallowed up in his. But her hand stayed steady, and again he had to admire that. The judge's words, issued in a deep, rumbling voice, were simply spoken and to the point. Vows and rings were exchanged in a matter of minutes, and then he pronounced them husband and wife.

His wife, Dev thought. He wasn't sure he'd ever really expected to have one. Just a week ago, he'd probably have said that "getting hitched," as the judge had put it, was the last thing on his mind. And now he was a married man. Some of the friends he'd had in his rowdier days would have roared at that.

"Time to kiss the bride," Judge Corbett told him with a sudden smile that lit up his broad face.

Dev knew he could hardly decline, even though Amanda was staring up at him with a faint frown knitting the creamy skin of her brow, as though having to see the ceremony through to its traditional end hadn't occurred to her before. Truth was, it hadn't occurred to him, either. But he wasn't going to look like a fool by stopping at this point. No way.

He could kiss her and get it done in no time, he told himself as he cupped his hands lightly around her shoulders. It would all be over in a matter of moments, he reflected with assurance, lowering his head.

Just a few seconds, he knew that's all it would take as he placed his lips on hers.

But he hadn't counted on how soft the pink-tinged mouth that had unaccountably fascinated him for some time would feel, how its silky smoothness would waste no time in reminding him that he hadn't kissed a woman in a while—and how certain parts of him would react. The most male parts of him.

He wasn't even aware that he had deepened the kiss until it was done. And then he was inside, touching, tasting and soon craving more—more of *this* woman. He wanted to reach around and remove the shiny clip that held her long hair back so he could run his fingers through it. He wanted to tug her closer until there wasn't a breath of space between them. He wanted…

Oh, yeah. Deep down in his gut, he knew he wanted it all.

But he couldn't have it. This was Amanda Bradley he was nearly ready to swallow whole. No, Amanda *Devlin.* Nonetheless, even if she had just become his wife, he had no business letting his libido take over. It was supposed to be a marriage in name only, nothing more. So he had to pull away. Reason told him that, and finally he managed to break the kiss.

Hauling in a long breath, he looked down at Amanda and released the grip he'd tightened on her shoulders. Rather than using her sudden freedom to step away, she continued to stare straight up at him. Only now her frown was gone and her eyes had widened.

In shock? he wondered. Somehow he didn't think so. No, she didn't look so much shocked as…astounded.

"Congratulations!" The judge gave Dev a bone-jarring slap on the back that would have felled a smaller man. "I just might have tried to kiss the bride, too, but I'd say you've already done a good job of it."

After a hearty laugh, he looked at Amanda. "What do you think, little lady?"

Chapter Four

What did she think? She thought something must be wrong with her. She thought her pulse was pounding far too hard and her brain had gone much too fuzzy. She thought that the world just might have, for a few endless moments, shifted into an entirely new realm, one where logic didn't rule.

It occurred to her that she wouldn't have been surprised if that theory turned out to be true, not surprised at all. In fact, it might be the only sensible explanation for what had happened—because she'd actually felt the stirrings of an unmistakable and undeniable response to Dev Devlin.

Dev Devlin!

"Looks like your new husband has left you speechless," Judge Corbett said, his tone amused.

Her husband. She would have to get used to hearing that, Amanda knew. But first she had to get herself together. "Not for long," she replied, making that as staunch a statement as she could. "I'm tougher than you think."

The judge laughed again. "Could be."

"Trust me, it's true," Dev muttered.

She ignored that comment. "I believe it's time to go."

He merely nodded his agreement, and they said goodbye to the judge. Leaving the stately brick courthouse that was a throwback to an earlier age, they returned to the parking lot.

"We've got time for a fast lunch before we head over to Family Services," Dev told her with a glance at a thick chrome watch that seemed to come with as many bells and whistles as his new Jeep.

Amanda had already made the appointment, but she hadn't told the authorities that she'd no longer be a single woman by the time she met with them. She could only imagine their reaction. It would probably at least raise some eyebrows when she arrived with a new groom in tow—a groom who'd done a thorough job of kissing the bride.

Why had he kissed her like that?

Amanda was still debating the matter when he spoke again. "I vote for a fast hamburger."

Her pulse still hadn't quite steadied, yet he seemed to have his mind on no more than food. Men, she thought. Could they all be this exasperating on occasion? "A salad," she said with the barest hint of irritation, "would be better for both of us."

He opened the passenger door. "If you say so." He looked down at her, his gaze bland. "Don't think I'm giving up my turn to have my way next so easily."

Amanda got in and waited for him to come around to the driver's side. While he reached in and tossed his hat on the back seat, she made a promise to herself to put all thoughts of that kiss straight out of her mind. She had more important things to think about.

"We need to decide on a strategy for this upcoming meeting," she told him as he revved the engine.

"I seem to remember mentioning that all you had to do was follow my lead," he countered, pulling out on the road.

She blew out a breath. "Easy enough for you to say, but where are you going?"

"To find a restaurant that looks salad friendly."

Her teeth clenched of their own accord. "I mean what tack do you intend to take when we get to Family Services?"

He tapped a finger on the steering wheel. "I plan to act like a newlywed—a real one."

And what exactly did that mean? she wondered. As one method occurred to her, she narrowed her eyes and fixed him with a steely stare. "No more kissing."

He shot her a look. "I wouldn't think of it. Although," he added as he went back to studying the road, "I've been told I'm not bad at it."

She didn't doubt that for a minute. The truth was, he was darn good at it. She wasn't an inexperienced woman. She'd been kissed plenty of times. During her years in Seattle, she'd dated several men and had very nearly become engaged to one of them. But something had held her back. For all that reason had said her suitor wasn't only a considerate lover but excellent husband and father material, as well, her less reasonable side had contended that he just wasn't Mr. Right. And for all that she'd enjoyed his kisses, she had to admit that he'd never kissed her as the man currently seated beside her had. No one had ever kissed her quite like that.

And here she was, Amanda realized, thinking about it when she'd vowed not to. Once more, she shoved it straight out of her mind. "Now make sure you keep it out," she told herself under her breath.

"Did you say something?" Dev asked.

"Nothing much." She rested her head against the back of the seat. "Let's just get lunch over with so we can head off to our meeting." Her stomach tightened at the thought of how important the next few hours were—for her and her sisters and brothers.

"Relax," Dev advised, as though he'd sensed how her nerves were threatening to take over. "We'll get through it and come out fine on the other end."

Amanda wanted to believe that, badly. Nevertheless, doubts continued to dog her. He didn't know—not nearly as well as she did, at any rate—that one of the people they'd be meeting with would be no pushover.

"I RECOGNIZE THE NAME, of course," Haynes McFadden said. The supervisor pursed his thin lips. "I dare say that in recent months most everyone in Pine Run has heard about the Main Street Millionaires."

Dev leaned back in a visitor's chair and propped his Stetson on an upraised knee. So the almost relentless media coverage that had gone on for weeks had turned out to do some good after all, he thought. He didn't have to convince anyone that he had a fat bank balance. "Then I'm sure you know that my wife and I—" he aimed a sidelong glance at Amanda, who sat next to him with her hands folded in her lap "—will have no problem giving the kids everything they need."

"Don't you own a saloon?" the fourth person in the room asked.

He looked toward where Louise Pearson stood next to her boss's desk. "I do."

He'd already latched on to the fact that if anyone had to be convinced of anything, it was this woman. *Impressive* was the best word he could come up with to describe her. Even dressed in a simple suit shaded a plain brown, she made an impact. It was, he decided, the way she had of looking at someone as if she could see clear down to their bones.

"Does that provide the right environment in which to raise four young children?" Again her question was blunt and to the point.

In contrast, Dev kept his tone mild. "They'd be living in a brand-new house that's nowhere near the bar. A big enough house, too, that each of them could have their own room."

"Well, I suppose a five-bedroom home would be fairly large," the supervisor allowed, his own voice politely calm.

"Actually there are six," Dev said. "We'd have a guest room, as well."

It didn't bother him that that was less than the truth. As far as he was concerned, it was nobody's business except his and Amanda's where they slept. What did bother him was the knowledge that it probably wouldn't be so easy for him to sleep under the same roof with her. Not after he'd had a taste of that silky soft mouth. It had been a mistake. Some parts of him might not think so, but his brain knew better.

The supervisor made some notes on a sheet of paper. "The housing situation can be verified, of course, but I don't feel that will be a problem. You clearly have the resources required to care for a large family. And you," he added, shifting his gaze to Amanda, "obviously care about your half siblings and want the best for them. I think Mrs. Pearson and I would both agree on that point."

The social worker dipped her head in a short nod. "That became apparent during the meeting with the children."

"I fell head over heels for them that day," Amanda admitted. "And I think they began to like me, too."

"I have to concede to having little doubt on both subjects." Louise's eagle-eyed gaze snapped back to Dev. "But I do have some questions about a few other things."

Why doesn't that surprise me? he reflected to himself even as he offered her a slow-as-molasses grin that had been known to win him success with the female half of the population. "Ask away," he invited.

Unfortunately his target didn't look in the least phased by his effort. "It seems to me," she said, "that this marriage happened rather quickly."

"It was an impulse," Dev agreed. "Once I proposed and Amanda said yes, I just couldn't wait."

Louise crossed her arms over the front of her suit jacket. "It appears that she wasn't expecting your proposal, since she made no mention of it when we last talked."

"Uh-huh." Dev issued a deep chuckle. "She was out-and-out stunned when I sprung it on her." He slid another look at Amanda. "Isn't that right… sweetheart?" *Just go along with me,* he told her with a silent stare.

Apparently getting the message, Amanda said, "I can honestly swear to being astonished."

Certain that, at least, was the perfect truth, Dev returned his gaze to Louise and tried out another grin.

"We've known each other for years, of course, and I knew she always had a soft spot in her heart for me—" he ignored the hasty cough that came from beside him "—but it wasn't until a few months ago, after I hit it big in the lottery and started to take a good look at my life, that I realized my true feelings for her."

Louise lifted a skeptical eyebrow. "But even then, you waited?"

"I had to." Dev assumed an earnest expression. "I wanted to have a house built first—the biggest and best house I could manage. As soon as it was ready just days ago—which you can confirm with the contractor, if you like—I popped the question."

Amanda shifted in her seat. God, he was good, was all she could think, even if he'd had her nearly choking with his comment about that soft spot in her heart for him. And, as strange as it seemed, the whole thing did sound reasonable as he'd described it, so reasonable she could almost believe it herself.

"Yes," she said, unable to resist a comment of her own, "he dropped down on one knee and all but begged me to marry him."

That won her another glance from the man at her side. The sudden glint in his gaze promised to get even for that whopper. "I didn't have to beg too hard, though, did I, sweetheart?"

She ran her tongue around her teeth, knowing she'd been neatly trapped. "I suppose not."

He turned his head to look straightforward and heaved a gusty sigh. "She's crazy about me."

The supervisor straightened his papers by tapping them on the desk. "Any more questions, Louise?"

The social worker shook her head. "I'll admit I

can't find any flaws in that explanation. And since I can't, I'm prepared to agree to having the necessary steps put in motion to place the children in the care of Mr. and Mrs. Devlin.''

Amanda let out a long breath. ''Thank you from the bottom of my heart,'' she said, and truly meant every word.

''This will, of course, still leave the children under the jurisdiction of this department,'' the supervisor reminded her. ''Formal adoption proceedings will have to be completed before you gain full custody.''

''I'll ask Mr. Whipple if he can start working on that,'' she told him, thinking that the elderly lawyer would probably be pleased as punch to take her on as a client. He knew how much she wanted the children. And now they were going to be hers! She wanted to jump up and hug everyone in the room, most especially the man who had married her in an effort to make this a reality.

No, don't go that far, wisdom said. *Better to offer your sunniest smile and keep your distance.*

Amanda didn't have to think twice about listening. Curving her lips widely, she rose and looked down at the man in question, not at all amazed when he returned her smile with what seemed to be a very satisfied one of his own. In complete charity with him for once, she wouldn't even have objected to his seeming a bit smug. As far as she was concerned, he deserved it.

She knew who was really responsible for the fact that she was one happy woman at the moment, and it was the very person she'd once regarded as her own personal pain in the posterior. Dev Devlin.

"How soon can we take the kids back to Jester?" he asked as he got to his feet.

"Since our questions have been answered to our satisfaction, I'll try to cut through the red tape," the supervisor told him. "Not much more than a week would be my estimation."

A week. Amanda could have struck up a dance at that news even as her practical side thought of the need to buy furniture for four more bedrooms. She was ready to pay for the extra expense out of her own pocket, but she imagined she'd be foiled in that regard. The new Devlin house was apparently at least partly furnished, and she had little doubt that its owner would insist on completing the job. That was where male pride came in, and she suspected he had his share.

Now that they'd be forced to spend time together, it would probably be wise to remember that in the coming days. She knew it could only be in the best interests of both of them to try to get along as well as they could, and the sooner they developed a friendlier relationship, the better—starting tonight.

Tonight. Amanda's smile faded as her nerves threatened to reassert themselves at the thought that she would no longer be occupying the small, cozy home so familiar to her. As a married woman, she was headed into uncharted territory, where she'd be living in a strange house, and sleeping in a new bed.

But how close would she and her new groom be sleeping to each other? That's what her nerves wanted to know.

AMANDA WAS STILL wondering about possible sleeping arrangements when she got her first good look at the Devlin house long after the sun had set. Even in the darkness, a silvery moon shining down joined forces with the soft glow of a nearby streetlamp to showcase a two-story frame home made of light pine. To Amanda, its rustic finish and modern design seemed a surprisingly good mix, one that featured plenty of wide windows below the steeply pitched shingled roof and a large front door lined on both sides with more gleaming glass.

Walking through that door, she found it was much the same inside, where bone-colored plastered walls with a rugged texture and bare of any decoration provided a backdrop for sturdy pine furniture built along contemporary lines.

"I'll give you the nickel tour in a minute," Dev said. His boot heels tapped on the polished wood floor as he led the way through the spacious living room toward a tall staircase set near the middle of the house. "We might as well get your suitcase stowed away first."

It didn't escape Amanda's notice that he handled the large piece of luggage as though it weighed nothing, which she knew was hardly the case, since she'd crammed it full in an effort to bring as many of her personal belongings as possible. Only a strong man could have managed it with ease, and this one seemed strong enough to have carried both it and his bride over the threshold with no trouble had he chosen to honor tradition.

Thankfully, he hadn't.

Amanda followed as he turned right at the top of the staircase. "There are three bedrooms on one side of the stairs and three on the other," he explained. "Yours is at the end of the hall here."

It didn't take Amanda long to conclude that the

room he'd referred to as hers was the master bedroom. Its size alone told her that. Again, the furniture it held was modern in style, including a pine bed large enough for her to get lost in—if she were sleeping here. Which, she assured herself, she wasn't.

"I'm not taking your bedroom," she said in no uncertain terms. "This is your house, and you belong here."

He set her suitcase down near a heavy dresser topped by a tall mirror and reached up to thumb back his wide-brimmed hat. "It makes more sense for you to stay here," he said, gesturing toward a closed door at one end of the room. "That leads to the smallest bedroom, where the littlest of the kids can sleep. With you here, you can keep an ear out for her."

She shook her head. "It may make sense, but it's not right. You should have the master bedroom."

"I don't think so." His jaw settled into a stubborn line. "The one at the other end of the house is the next biggest, and that's plenty of space for me."

"Not as I see it."

"But it's my turn to get my way," he said, arching a brow.

That statement had her frowning in a heartbeat. She knew she'd lost, because she'd already agreed to go along with that plan for compromise, and she kept her word. But she didn't have to like it. "Okay, I'll stay here, but I'm saving my turn to use to good advantage."

"Fine." If that warning worried him, it didn't show. "Why don't you hang up your coat and we'll go over the rest of the house?"

She hung her raincoat on an empty rack in a closet nearly the size of her old bedroom and poked her head into a connecting bath that turned out to be several sizes bigger than the one she was used to. It all but screamed for some color, with most everything in sight, including the thick towels, a sparkling white. Nevertheless, it was…dazzling.

"Good Lord," she said, "you could hold a party in the tub alone."

A low chuckle came from behind her. "Now why didn't I think of that?"

She turned and found that his blue eyes had taken on more than a hint of amusement. He was enjoying his newly acquired wealth, that was pretty plain. It came as little surprise, since from what she'd heard of the Devlin family, he'd grown up with few of the conveniences he could now readily afford. The irony of it was that, while she herself had grown up in a comfortably middle-class household, even a very happy one before her father had disappeared from her life, he seemed more at ease with the luxuries currently at his command.

Then again, Dev Devlin had had several months to get used to being a millionaire. She was still groping to take in the fact that she'd become the wife of one.

"I'm ready for the tour you mentioned," she said with all the briskness she could muster.

"Right this way." With that, he offered an oh-so-polite bow from the waist, displaying a smooth yet forceful command of his body soon duplicated by a large black cat that met them in the hallway.

"This is Rufus," Dev said by way of introduction. "He used to mostly hang out in my room behind the saloon. Now he's got a whole house to roam around in, and I never know where he'll pop out from."

Amanda bent and held a hand out, but Rufus kept

his distance. "I suppose he'll have to get comfortable with me."

"Uh-huh." Dev reached down to run his fingers over the cat's back, which immediately produced a loud purr. "Don't be surprised if it takes a while. He was mainly skin and bones when I came across him looking for a meal and doing his best to pry the lid off a garbage can a few summers back. Even after I began feeding him regularly, it took some time before he started cozying up to me."

She straightened. "It certainly seems as though he's eating well now."

"There's plenty meat on those bones," Dev agreed. He gave the cat a last rub and gestured to an open doorway. "That's the hall entrance to the smallest bedroom. Nothing in the room now, but we'll fix that before the kids get here."

After one look, Amanda had to judge it perfect for the littlest of the Bradley bunch. And the empty bedroom across the hall next to a second bath would fit another of the children, she decided as the tour continued. "As the eldest," she said, "Liza seems protective of the younger children. I think she'd be more comfortable if she was as close to Betsy as possible."

"I can't say I'm all that familiar with kids, but I guess it makes sense," Dev allowed as they headed for the other side of the center staircase, the cat leading the way.

"These bedrooms should suit the boys to a *T*," Amanda told him after poking her head into the first two rooms they came to. Another bath came next, and then the last bedroom on the far end of the hall. His bedroom. She held back a sigh that might have spelled

relief at the thought that at least their rooms were nowhere near each other.

His was furnished in much the same fashion as the
master bedroom, she noted, glancing around while he
took off his hat and suit jacket and tossed them on an
overstuffed chair. Like the twin chairs in the biggest
bedroom, plus the assortment of chairs and long sofa
in the living room, it was covered in a natural-colored
fabric framed by light wood. "For some reason," she
said, tucking her tongue in her cheek, "I'm beginning
to suspect that you have a love affair with pine."

He loosened his tie. "The truth is, I wasn't sure
what went with what, so I just ordered everything to
match."

The admission came with such a rueful slant of his
mouth that it made her laugh out loud for the first time
in what seemed like far too long. "I think you did a
good job."

His eyebrows winged up. "A compliment from the
woman who looked about ready to strangle me on a
few occasions? I never thought I'd see the day."

"I believe in giving credit where credit is due," she
said before reminding herself that it might not be wise
to be too agreeable. Yes, for everyone's sake, she
wanted to further a friendlier relationship, but… She
crossed her arms under her breasts. "But I'm still no
pushover…Mr. Macho."

He narrowed his gaze just slightly, just enough to
tell her that the hardly complimentary nickname she
hadn't used since a truce had been silently declared
could still produce a response. "I'll do my best to
remember that…Ms. Prim."

Ms. Prim. Dev clasped his hands behind his head and
stared up at a bedroom ceiling painted gleaming white,

thinking he'd be a lot better off if he could still consider the woman sleeping under his roof for the first time to be one prim and proper female. Trouble was, he knew more about her now, including a preference for novels with covers leaving little doubt as to their sexy subject matter. Not to mention his recent discovery that, for a small person, she packed a wallop when it came to kissing, more than enough to qualify her as experienced.

"Cripes, how's a man suppose to just ignore the whole thing?" he grumbled to himself.

In reply, he got a low growl from the cat curled up at the foot of the bed.

"If that was a warning to watch my step before I go off the deep end," he told his companion, muttering into the murky darkness all around him, "you could damn well be right."

Dev frowned as it occurred to him that he just might have an easier time keeping his thoughts from wandering to places they had no business going if Amanda Bradley—no, Amanda *Devlin*—hadn't looked as though she fit his new home like a glove when he'd been showing her around. But, for some reason, she had. It was almost as if, as he'd done his best to lead Family Services to believe, he'd built the place with her in mind.

Which was flat-out ridiculous, he knew.

For all that he'd paid top dollar for the house and everything in it, it was nowhere near as fancy as her bookstore. Or as cozy as the small house she owned, for that matter. Only a blind man would contend otherwise. Whatever tall tales he'd told to a sharp-eyed social worker earlier that day, the simple truth was that he'd built and furnished his place to suit him. Period. It had to be a fluke that Amanda had looked right at home in it.

And maybe she wouldn't tomorrow. Maybe when they faced each other over the breakfast table, he'd find out that it was only his imagination working overtime. Maybe all he needed was a good night's rest to have him discovering that he'd been all wet.

Dev punched up a pillow and turned over on his side. As he closed his eyes, a cool breeze drifted in from the window he'd left open a crack, reminding him that he had to get some drapes up so he wouldn't have to keep turning out the lights before getting undressed. Right now, if he stripped down to the bare skin he preferred to spend his nights in without remembering that little detail, he risked shocking the new neighbors he was out to impress with his respectability.

The problem was, he had no clue as to what kind of drapes to buy. He supposed he'd just have to pick out something or other and hope for the best.

"Or," he said, his eyes flashing open as another, and unmistakably pleasing, thought hit, "I could just leave it to someone else."

Below him, the cat shifted and offered another low growl, but Dev scarcely heard it as he began to mull over at least one benefit that might well come his way as the result of the day's events. A big benefit, as far as he was concerned, because he wouldn't have to deal with picking out colors and fabrics and God knows what. Not anymore.

He had a wife who could decorate the rest of the place. With any luck at all, he'd only have to pay the bills and tell her that whatever she thought was up to snuff was okay with him. He wouldn't have to make any more of the kind of decisions that drove him crazy—provided she agreed to go along with it.

Dev smiled to himself, thinking that if he played his cards right, she probably would. If he eased around to asking her to do it, instead of confronting her with the project head-on, that could be his ticket to success, and then he'd be able to watch his house get whatever it still needed to put it in topnotch shape without doing it himself. Which, he figured, just might be every style-challenged male's idea of heaven.

"It's definitely worth a shot," he muttered under his breath.

But first they had to get through the uproar that seemed bound to hit tomorrow. Jaws may have already stopped dropping, thanks to the brief phone call Amanda had made late that afternoon to break the news of the wedding to Irene Caldwell, but a storm of tongue-wagging might not be far behind.

Whatever was headed their way, the newlyweds had to be ready to form a united front and convince Jester's sure-to-be-skeptical residents that their marriage was the real, genuine thing. And then they had to keep them believing it until there was no chance that Amanda's sisters and brothers could be taken away from her.

Starting tomorrow, Dev knew, he and Amanda would have to put on quite a show.

Chapter Five

"I can't believe it."

Amanda wasn't sure who had issued that statement. It could have been any of the women crowded into the sitting area at the rear of the bookstore. Not that it mattered, she thought. The Ex-Libris had been open for less than an hour, and it seemed as if she'd already heard endless variations on the same theme.

I never would have so much as imagined it.

You could have knocked me over with a feather when I heard about it.

Goodness gracious, it can't be true!

So far, she'd done her best to assure her visitors that her marriage was indeed a reality. And, so far, most were still shaking their heads in wonder. She was gearing up to give it another try when a new arrival appeared on the scene. The last time she'd seen Shelly O'Rourke, the nicely curved woman with chin-length hair in a rich shade of dark brown had been happily looking forward to accompanying her husband on a trip to San Francisco, and to becoming a new mother in several months' time.

Now, Shelly didn't look so much happy as... flabbergasted.

"I didn't expect you back for a couple more days," Amanda said.

"Connor's conscience began to nag him about being away from the clinic for too long, so we headed home early. And what *I* didn't expect," Shelly added, "was to walk into The Brimming Cup this morning and find out that my good friend had stunned my employees, not to mention everyone else buzzing like a swarm of bees in the coffee shop, by getting married."

"And to Dev Devlin," Wyla Thorpe tacked on with a soft snort. Her mouth, shaded a bright red to match her short hair, turned down at the corners in the typically sour expression she'd done little to hide for months. Wyla had decided against contributing any more to the weekly lottery just days before the other regular players had come into a small fortune, and the string-bean-thin woman in her forties who favored wearing tight polyester to apparently make herself look even thinner seldom hesitated to display her displeasure at losing out.

"Yes, the man Amanda picked is what really makes it so unbelievable," another of the women said, and a round of hastily murmured agreements followed.

"I thought so, too," Irene Caldwell admitted from her spot on one of the twin love seats. "At least I did when she called me yesterday to break the news. But last night something occurred to me that changed my way of thinking."

That statement won everyone's attention in a hurry, including Amanda's. She leaned one hip against a small mahogany cabinet that held the delicate china cups and saucers she used to serve complimentary tea to her customers and gazed down at Irene, wondering what the older woman could possibly have in mind.

Fortunately she didn't have to wait more than a moment before Regina Larson, the mayor's middle-aged wife, jumped into the conversation. Standing near the doorway to a small rear bathroom, she dipped her dyed-blond head to fix Irene with a puzzled frown. "What in the world are you talking about? Amanda and Dev Devlin have been at odds for who knows how long."

"Yes," Irene agreed as a slow smile bloomed on her face. "But that was before he *saved* her."

Amanda blinked. Whatever she might have anticipated, it wasn't that.

"Saved her?" Shelly repeated from where she stood steps beyond the last in a row of tall bookshelves, looking as mystified as many of the others in the store.

"You've been away," Irene told her, "so you probably haven't heard that Dev Devlin came to Amanda's rescue when she was almost assaulted right on the bookstore's doorstep one evening by that awful drifter, Guy Feldon."

"No, I hadn't heard." Shelly wasted no time in redirecting her gaze to Amanda. Her hazel eyes hadn't lost that baffled look, but she said nothing more.

Instead, it was Regina who spoke again as she assumed a thoughtful expression. "Now that you mention it, Irene, I do remember someone telling me about how the two men had actually come to blows."

Several other heads nodded, as though more of the group were recalling the incident, as well.

Irene's smile grew. "In a way, he became her knight in shining armor that evening, and I believe it may well have been the beginning of a transformation in their relationship." She glanced up at the woman who, at least as far as Irene was plainly concerned, had been a damsel in distress until a romantic rescue had been achieved. "Am I right?" she asked brightly.

"I suppose you could say so," Amanda replied after a moment, realizing it was the truth—or partly, anyway. That evening, she and the Heartbreaker Saloon's owner had gone beyond the shaky truce they'd formed and started talking, which in turn had led to an undeniable change in their relationship. Not a wildly romantic one, true. But a change, nonetheless.

"Sounds a little fanciful to me," Wyla said. She crossed her arms over her narrow chest and leaned back in her seat on one of the plump leather chairs.

No one was impolite enough to point out that someone twice divorced, and the last time after a nasty court battle that had left her with one of the most prosperous farms in the area, might not be the best judge of how happy endings could be achieved.

"Why don't I make some tea?" Amanda suggested, deciding a bid to switch subjects was in order. "Gwen should be here soon with her pastries."

Just then, as if right on cue, the front door opened and Gwendolyn Tanner carried in a large plastic container filled with the baked goods she regularly delivered. Like Shelly, Gwen continued to run a business—in Gwen's case, the only boarding house in town—even though, in both instances, money was no longer a driving concern, thanks to their lottery win. Rather than pay Gwen for the baking she continued to do for the love of it, Amanda made a regular donation to one of Gwen's favorite charities, and that had come to suit them both.

"Hello, everyone," Gwen said as the group parted so she could set her burden on the low, cloth-covered table that stood between the love seats. Raising a hand to smooth back a stray strand of auburn hair confined in a neat, upswept style, Gwen looked at Amanda and offered her particular brand of a wide yet almost shyly sweet smile. "Why am I not surprised to find a crowd here?" she asked, straightening the bottom edge of the heavy, loosely fitted yellow sweater she wore with cotton slacks.

Before her win, Gwen had been as slender as a reed. During the past couple of months, however, it hadn't escaped Amanda's notice that the enthusiastic baker had been putting on some weight, and more than a few pounds. She'd begun to wonder if anyone else was growing as curious about that fact as she was. Still, since it was hardly any of her business, she'd kept that curiosity to herself.

"They're probably a hungry crowd," Amanda replied as lightly as she could. And even if they weren't, she thought to herself, she was going to feed them. At least as long as their mouths were full, they wouldn't be asking any more questions about her marriage. With that goal in mind, she pulled out a silver tray she kept behind the cabinet holding tea supplies.

"I'll put the pastries out for you," Irene offered, sitting forward to take the tray.

"Thanks." Although far from hungry herself, having fixed a large breakfast for the first time in as long as she could remember, Amanda ran her tongue over her lips. "As usual, those pastries look delicious, Gwen," she said as Irene began her task with a golden creation topped by a sprinkling of powdered sugar.

"Being a newlywed must work up an appetite," someone in the back of the group offered with dry humor.

Amanda ignored that remark, and the few titters that

followed. Despite the fact that she could have done without both, her more practical side told her it was better to have people making pointed comments about her wedding night rather than the hasty ceremony itself. They had no way of knowing that she'd slept alone only to wake up surprisingly refreshed after a final string of restless nights as a single woman. It was as if she'd been able to relax at last.

Not, she had to admit, that there'd been anything very relaxing about sharing breakfast with her new groom. But even then, as he'd all but wolfed down the cheese omelet she'd offered to fix while he made coffee, her nerves had mostly taken the whole thing in stride—a major accomplishment, since the coffee he'd produced was strong enough to have her eyelids standing at attention after one sip.

Her nerves might have done even better if he hadn't looked far too good wearing just a T-shirt and jeans.

"Well," Gwen said, regaining Amanda's attention, "although I have to confess to probably being as stunned as everyone else, I'd like to offer my congratulations."

Amanda couldn't hold back a smile. "Thank you," she said, her tone as sincere as Gwen's had been. She'd always felt that this woman was one of the nicest people in Jester, and that, as far as Amanda was concerned, had just been confirmed. "How about staying for some tea and maybe a pastry?"

Gwen shook her head. "No, I really have to be going."

"Goodness knows," Wyla murmured just loud enough to be heard, "she doesn't need any more calories."

Gwen flushed as the store turned starkly silent.

She obviously hadn't been the only one to notice, Amanda thought. And now Gwen's feelings had been trounced on. "I don't see that what a person does or doesn't eat is anyone's concern but theirs," she said.

"Right on," Shelly seconded, her voice firm.

Suddenly Gwen threw up an exasperated hand. "Oh, what's the use. It's pretty plain that most of you have been speculating about me. Well, you know what? I have been putting on weight, and it's not because I'm stuffing myself." She paused and aimed her gaze around the group. "It's because I'm pregnant."

More silence, even starker than before, followed hard on the heels of that announcement. Amanda was all but certain of the single thought foremost on everyone's mind. *Shy, quiet Gwen who didn't even seem to date much was pregnant?*

Irene made a sound of distress. It was no secret that she was as fond as a grandmother might be of someone she'd gotten close to while living at the boarding house. "Gwen, dear—" she began, only to halt in midword as Gwen shook her head.

"There's probably another thing most of you have just started to wonder about, so I might as well get this all said at once." Again Gwen paused. "I'm not only pregnant...*I don't know who the father is.*" And with those ringing words, she turned on a dime and marched out of the store.

Now the group wasn't only stunned but clearly shocked.

"I have to go to her," Irene said, rising. She was the first out the door, but it wasn't long before the newest sensation had Amanda's marriage coming in a distant second as other members of the group left in rapid succession. In a matter of moments, only Amanda and Shelly remained.

"I don't think I can take any more news bulletins today," Shelly said as she sank into one of the newly vacant chairs.

Following her example, Amanda sat on the nearest love seat. "Let's hope the rest of the morning goes better for both of us."

Shelly folded her arms across the front of her quilted pink jacket. "I'll go along with that—provided it doesn't mean you're hoping I'll just accept Irene's explanation for your quick trip down the aisle with Dev Devlin." She looked her friend straight in the eye. "Now, do you want to give me the real scoop on that, or do I have to try to pry it out of you?"

Amanda told herself she should have known better than to think for even one second that Shelly would just let it drop. And that being the case, she knew she had two choices. She could simply refuse to discuss the whole thing, or she could take Shelly into her confidence. Either way, their longtime friendship would survive. Amanda was sure of that. But she couldn't deny that she was tempted to confide in another woman, and none was as close to her as this one.

"All right," she said, "I'll come clean. Just be prepared for some more surprises."

"Thanks for the warning." Shelly took a deep breath. "Okay, I'm ready."

"It all started when I received a phone call from a lawyer in Pine Run." With that, Amanda began to explain the events leading up to her marriage, holding nothing back except the circumstances surrounding her father's death; she remained determined to keep those details private. As she approached the end of her story, she also left out the fact that her new groom had kissed his bride witless seconds after the ceremony was over. She wasn't letting anyone know how much that kiss had affected her, not even Shelly. And especially not *him.*

"You weren't kidding about more surprises," Shelly said when Amanda finished. "Four newly discovered half siblings would have been enough. But then Dev offering to marry you so you could gain custody really tops it off."

"I nearly keeled over when he did," Amanda admitted.

Shelly smiled a small smile. "I can just imagine."

"Of course," Amanda added, "it's not a marriage in the ordinary sense of the word."

"I suppose not, since you both seem to have agreed it will be in name only." Shelly hesitated a beat. "Still, that sort of relationship might not be so easy to maintain."

Amanda frowned. "What do you mean?"

Her friend lifted one shoulder in a shrug. "He's a man. You're a woman. Whatever arguments you've had in the past have had to be set aside. And you'll be living together."

"But sleeping separately," Amanda pointed out.

"Plus there's the sheer truth that he's darn good-looking," Shelly continued as though Amanda hadn't spoken. "Now that you two have joined forces, who knows what it could lead to."

"I'll tell you what it won't lead to, and that's the two of us growing old together," Amanda said with assurance.

It was Shelly's turn to frown. "Why are you so certain of that?"

Amanda countered with a question of her own. "Do you honestly think that Dev Devlin is the type to ever really settle down—not just for a few months, or even a few years, but for a lifetime?"

Shelly mulled that over for a minute. "I wouldn't have thought so," she said at last. "I'd certainly have to agree that he seemed content living a bachelor's life."

"Yes, and he'll probably be content to go back to it after the adoption is final and my sisters and brothers have a secure future."

"Maybe," Shelly conceded. "I suppose that remains to be seen." Once again her smile broke through. "When do the kids get here?"

"It could be in as little as a week, the authorities said." Amanda straightened in her seat. "And speaking of the authorities, I don't believe I've mentioned yet that Louise Pearson is the social worker assigned to the case."

Shelly's smile took a wry slant, as though she had no trouble recalling how she'd found herself dealing with the same social worker months earlier. "It won't be easy to put anything over on her."

"I've already discovered that," Amanda said in a rueful tone. "At the moment, Family Services thinks my marriage is a love match, so that has to be the official version as far as most people in Jester are concerned, too."

Shelly nodded her agreement. "How do you plan to break the news about the children?"

"As simply and quietly as possible."

"Not like your wedding announcement, hmm?" Shelly asked with a twinkle in her eye.

Amanda had to laugh. It was either that or groan.

"Thank goodness no one got around to commenting on the lack of a honeymoon."

"Uh-huh. They all probably got a good look at your ring, though." Shelly leaned forward and studied the object in question. "It must have made quite an impression. Heaven knows, it's impressing me."

Amanda dropped her gaze to the beautiful diamond ring that, as it had more than once by now, seemed to wink back at her. "He didn't have to buy me this."

"But he did. And I'm assuming he picked it out." At Amanda's nod, Shelly said, "Your husband has good taste."

Her husband. Amanda wasn't sure she'd ever get used to hearing that. "He does," she had to agree.

She also had to wonder what the man she'd married would have to deal with once the Heartbreaker Saloon opened its doors.

I'D HAVE EXPECTED hell to freeze over first.

My mouth fell halfway to my feet when I got the news.

Jumping Jehoshaphat, it can't be true!

Those comments—just a sample of all he'd heard from the minute the first of a steady stream of customers had started showing up at noon—continued to echo in Dev's mind as he walked home from the Heartbreaker early that evening. He could only be grateful that he'd planted those earlier seeds with his head bartender, who'd been the sole person to admit to not being flat-out amazed by recent events.

"I figured something was up," Roy had said, nodding his head wisely. "The signs were there, if a man looked hard enough."

That had produced several thoughtful expressions,

as if some of the bar's regular clientele were wondering what they'd missed. Dev chose to take it as a welcome indication that things just might start to settle down soon, enough anyway so that he'd no longer have to dodge nonstop questions about his marriage.

And at least being married had given him an excuse to get away for a few hours. "Told my wife I'd be home for dinner," he'd announced before leaving. A roar of laughter had gone up at that news, followed by some suggestive comments as he'd shoved his way out through the bar's swinging doors. His bride probably wouldn't have appreciated them, but then, if she'd been around none of those remarks would have seen the light of day.

Dev was sure of that. As far as most folks in Jester were concerned, Amanda was still a real lady, even if her new husband had never laid claim to being a refined gentleman.

The appetizing aroma of something cooking greeted him as he let himself into the house. He doubted it came from a frozen tray popped into the microwave— his most tried-and-true method of producing a meal when he played chef. He left his hat and jacket in the entryway closet, then let his nose lead him down a long hallway toward the kitchen at the rear of the house.

His wife was there, standing at the brand-new, state-of-the-art, stainless-steel stove, where one of the shiny new skillets he'd bought at Main Street's biggest store, The Mercantile, was sizzling away.

"Something smells good," he said, leaning a shoulder against one side the arched doorway. *Much to my surprise,* he could have added. He and Amanda had agreed that, since most people would probably expect it of newlyweds, it would be smart to have dinner together as often as possible. But he hadn't been prepared to find her cooking up a storm, even though she'd fixed a tasty breakfast for both of them.

He also hadn't expected to see her wearing a casual top and khaki pants. That morning, she'd come downstairs dressed in one of her silky blouses paired with a slim skirt, every inch the take-charge businesswoman. Now she looked…younger, he decided. Maybe even more approachable, somehow.

Still, he didn't take that for a minute to mean she'd welcome another kiss. Not from him. Even as she turned and offered a small smile, he was sure on that score.

"What smells good is stir-fry," she told him. "I bought some fresh vegetables at the Stop 'N' Shop after I closed up the bookstore."

"Never thought about those when I stocked the refrigerator last weekend," he admitted.

Her smile widened just a bit. "I noticed."

He straightened from the doorway and ambled into the room. Per instructions, the contractor had gone all out to fill it with broad counters, tall cabinets and top-of-the-line appliances, all lit by a string of high windows that overlooked the large yard.

"Do you plan on cooking dinner every night?" he asked.

She turned back to the skillet. "If you'll handle the clean-up, I'll take on the job most nights."

"Deal."

That won him a quick glance over her shoulder. "Sure you don't want to think about it?"

"Uh-huh. Not unless you plan on cooking only vegetables."

"I know how to cook lots of things," she assured him.

"Barbecue?"

"Yes. But I think I'll leave that to you and the huge grill I spied out on the rear deck."

"Damn," Dev muttered.

She flicked off the stove burner. "Thought you might get away without cooking entirely, did you?"

He heaved a gusty sigh. "A man has his dreams."

"So," Amanda told him with another small smile, "does a woman. In my case, while I like to cook, I can generally do without housecleaning."

Dev aimed a glance around him. "No doubt about the fact that this is a lot of house to clean. After dinner, I think we'd better talk about hiring some help. An outside service could probably do the bulk of the cleaning, but we've also got to have someone to look after the kids while we're both at work."

"I have to confess to hoping it won't be necessary for me to stop working entirely," she acknowledged. "Nonetheless, I'm prepared to do whatever I have to when it comes to the children, including closing the Ex-Libris."

"Even if it's going to hurt like hell," he said, sure of his words. By now, he had a good handle on how much the place meant to her, and the upshot was that whatever thoughts he'd had about expanding his business at the cost of hers were fast disappearing. He'd never laid claim to being a sensitive man, but that didn't mean he couldn't sympathize with how she felt. Then, too, he could still pursue his idea of making some improvements to the Heartbreaker without the added space, and he supposed they'd come up with a way to make sure she could continue to run her own business, as well, although that might take some doing.

He heaved another sigh. "Don't worry, we'll figure something out to solve our problems on the home and work front."

Her gaze met his. "Are you beginning to have second thoughts about this whole thing?"

"No," he replied with total honesty. He'd made a commitment to keep four kids safe and he was sticking to it. "Now," he continued, offering a wry smile of his own in a bid to lighten the mood, "do I have to just keep smelling dinner, or are you going to feed me?"

SHE FED HIM. They sat at a round, glassed-top table in the breakfast nook taking up one large corner of the kitchen. Despite the casualness of the setting, there was room enough to easily seat six, while the long pine table holding center stage under a sleek metal chandelier in the spacious dining room off the hall would accommodate twice that many.

But for all of the dining space available in the house, Amanda had failed to find either a tablecloth or so much as a single placement during an earlier search. She'd been forced to settle for two double sheets of paper towels to hold the heavy white stoneware plates and shiny silverware she'd retrieved from the kitchen cabinets.

Even being a millionaire, she thought with some amusement, hadn't transformed the man seated across from her into the kind of person who considered proper table linens as much a part of the meal as the food being served. A person like her own mother, Amanda had to concede, remembering how she herself had been raised to value the small trimmings that added a personal touch to almost any setting.

What had her husband's—yes, she had to start thinking of him that way—mother been like? Amanda couldn't help but wonder. Along with most of the town's longer-term residents, she knew his father had worked at the slaughterhouse in Pine Run, and that both his parents had died of exposure when they'd been stranded in their old pickup on a snowy road during a particularly potent winter storm a few years after Amanda had arrived in Jester. They'd left two sons behind, Dev and his older brother. While Dev had remained in Jester, his brother had long since departed.

"I've got to admit this is pretty tasty," Dev remarked as he forked up another slice of the boneless chicken breast she'd mixed in with the vegetables.

"Thanks." Amanda waited a second, then asked, "Was your mother a good cook?"

"Not especially," he said after a beat. And that was all he said before lifting his water glass for a short swallow.

She toyed with a small spear of broccoli. "Do you ever hear from your brother?"

"No." He offered a thin strip of chicken to the cat stretched out at his feet and received a grateful purr in return.

"How about your uncle?"

"Not since he hightailed it out of town after I bought the Heartbreaker from him."

He went back to concentrating on his dinner, leaving Amanda to come to the swift conclusion that he had no desire to talk about his family. Knowing it was his choice, she dropped the subject, and silence reigned for several moments before she spoke again. "Shelly and Connor came back from their trip early. She stopped by the bookstore this morning, right along with what seemed like half the female population of Jester."

"The Heartbreaker had more than its share of visitors, too," Dev assured her. "The doors were barely open when they started showing up."

"I can imagine." Amanda set her fork down and reached for her iced tea, deciding it was only fair that she pass along some more news. "I think you should know that after the rest of the crowd left, I told Shelly the reason behind our getting married. She agreed to keep it to herself."

"Which means she will," he said with a confident nod. "I can't deny she's been a friend to both of us, even though she must have sometimes felt like she was between a rock and a hard place."

The apt description of what Shelly had undoubtedly had to deal with on more than one occasion made Amanda laugh. "I suppose that's true."

Not for the world did she plan to so much as mention Shelly's theory that Dev Devlin just might be too attractive for her good friend to live with on a day-to-day—or, more likely, night-to-night—basis and resist on a man-woman level. Well, Shelly was mistaken, Amanda told herself as she returned to her meal. *But not about his being attractive,* an inner voice contended. She ignored it and speared another piece of chicken.

"Since you had a freezer full of ice cream, I thought we'd have that for dessert," she said when they'd both polished their plates clean—his after two heaping helpings.

"Ice cream always works. I'll get rid of this stuff first." True to the deal they'd made, he cleared off the table while she relaxed. Working with a smooth efficiency she had to admire, he was loading the large dishwasher when the front doorbell rang.

"I'll get it," she offered, rising.

"If it's anyone with another stack of questions about our marriage," he grumbled, "just tell them we're too busy to satisfy their curiosity."

Her lips curved. "After today, I'm almost ready to do that."

"So do it," he said as she started for the doorway to the hall. "And if that doesn't put a lid on it, tell them dinner's over and I was gearing up to make love to you on top of the kitchen table. That should have them leaving in a hurry."

She came to a dead halt. "I think that's going a bit far," she replied after taking a moment to regroup. Then, without so much as a backward glance, she walked out of the kitchen, reminding herself that there was no reason for her pulse to take off on its own. He'd only been joking. *He had to be joking.* And the joke would be on her if she let it affect her.

Amanda opened the door and found herself being greeted by two beaming faces belonging to a couple who could have doubled for Mr. and Mrs. Santa Claus—white hair, roly-poly bodies and all. "Welcome to the neighborhood," they said in unison.

She recognized Ike and Mabel Murphy, although she'd never had much occasion to speak to them before, other than nodding a hello or sharing a comment about the weather when they'd bumped into each other in the shops everyone in town frequented.

"I didn't realize you lived on Maple Street," Amanda said.

"Actually, we live right next door," Ike told her. "In the small blue house with the white trim."

"And we thought it only fitting to bring you a little something," Mabel added, "especially since I had my hair done at the Crowning Glory today and heard all the excitement about your wedding." She extended a square baking plan covered with foil. "They're brownies—fresh from the oven."

"Thank you." Amanda took the offering and stepped back. "Please come in. I know my…husband will want to thank you, too." Satisfied that she'd gotten the word out with only a brief hesitation, she summoned a smile.

"Well, just for a minute," Mabel said as she walked in. "We know you newlyweds must want to be alone."

Choosing to ignore that brightly issued remark, Amanda brought her visitors back to the kitchen, with Mabel oohing and aahing all the way. "You have an impressive house," the older woman soon told both Devlins.

"Mighty fine," Ike seconded as the two men shook hands.

"Appreciate your thinking so," Dev said. At his invitation, the couple took a seat at the glass-topped table.

Ike stroked his bushy white beard. "We noticed you coming by to check on the progress as the place was being built."

Dev hid a wry grin at that, because he'd done some noticing of his own. The frilly curtains in the house next door had parted more than once during his regular trips.

"Mabel brought us some homemade brownies," Amanda told him, dropping a glance down at the pan she held.

He nodded and leaned a hip against the counter. "Guess we can have those for dessert with our ice cream."

"Yes." Amanda set the pan next to him and removed a layer of foil. Immediately the sweet scent of fresh baking filled the air. "Please feel free to join us," she told the Murphys.

They traded glances before Ike asked, "Are you sure you two want company?"

Amanda looked at Dev. "Of course. We just finished dinner and were planning to discuss getting some household help. But that can wait, can't it?"

No mention of his comment about making love on the table, Dev noted. Not that he expected one. The grin he'd held back broke through. "Whatever you say…sweetheart."

Mabel sighed. "It's so wonderful to see young love in bloom."

After a second of sheer silence, Amanda wasted no time in saying, "I'll get some plates." She turned and started toward one of the cabinets. "Will you get the ice cream…dear?"

"Uh-huh." Dev did as instructed, and in a matter of moments they pulled out padded chrome chairs and joined the older couple.

Dev scooped up a spoonful of warm chocolate brownie paired with a side of rapidly melting vanilla and moaned after the first swallow. It was either that or purr like Rufus, who'd abandoned a spot near the table for what the cat probably considered a cautious distance. "This is downright delicious," he told Mabel.

She laughed, a tinkling sound. "That's what Ike says every time he talks me into making brownies."

"I don't have to talk too hard," Ike remarked around his own hefty scoop of dessert. "She's always baking something."

"And we're both eating it." Mabel patted her stomach. "Which is why we've gained weight since we retired and sold our farm a few years back."

"Nothing like tramping through a corn field to keep you fit," Ike agreed.

Mabel released another sigh. "What I need is something to keep me busy. Once it starts to warm up in earnest, Ike will have plenty to keep him occupied with his garden in the backyard. I enjoy my quilting, but it's not enough."

"Do you do much reading?" Amanda asked.

Mabel shook her head. "I never developed the habit, which is why you haven't seen me in your store."

"What she's really into," Ike said with a fond look at his wife, "is riding herd on kids and generally acting like a mother hen, except ours left the nest a long time ago. Now they live out of state—and all our grandkids, too."

Well, before much longer a bunch of kids would be living practically on their doorstep, Dev thought. Except they didn't know it yet. He slid a sidelong glance at Amanda and found her watching him with a thoughtful expression, as though her mind was running along the same lines. This could be a good time to ease into breaking the news about her half siblings. At least that was his take on it. Still, he was leaving it up to her, something he tried to convey with a meaningfully lifted brow.

After a moment she dipped her head in a short nod, then turned her attention back to Mabel. "Since you seem to be fond of children, you may be glad to hear that you'll soon have some for neighbors." Amanda followed up that statement with a brief explanation.

The grandmotherly woman beamed. "I certainly am glad to hear it. And if you need any help with them, just let me know."

Dev and Amanda exchanged another pointed look before she spoke with slow deliberation. "Maybe, if you're willing, we could try to work something out, Mabel."

And that was how Dev came to be whistling a satisfied tune as he headed back to the Heartbreaker less than an hour later. Things were shaping up, he thought. With an outside service to deal with the cleaning, and Mabel Murphy eager to take on the job of part-time nanny and earn herself a good wage in the process, he and Amanda could leave those problems behind and concentrate on getting the house ready for the kids.

Would they like the place? Dev wondered. Not much reason why they shouldn't, he decided. No, all things considered, he had little doubt on that score. Then another question surfaced.

Would they like *him?*

Dev frowned as he continued on his way. This time, he was a lot less sure of the answer.

Chapter Six

"We're almost there," Amanda told her four passengers. "That's Jester straight up ahead."

"It doesn't look very big," Liza offered in a quiet voice from the rear seat, where she sat with Patrick and Betsy.

"You're right," Amanda agreed, keeping a cautious eye on the road ahead. She was still getting used to driving a larger vehicle, having traded in her gray compact for a sandy beige minivan just days earlier. The man she'd married had, somewhat predictably, wanted to buy her a brand-new model, one that came with all the bells and whistles, but she'd dug in her heels and insisted that a used van would be more than adequate. She'd had to give up her turn to have her way in the effort, after which he'd wasted no time in having his when it came to furnishing the children's bedrooms far beyond the bare necessities. *Extravagant* was the only word that came to mind, since four once-empty rooms were now almost filled to capacity.

"Why did they call the town Jester?" Caleb wanted to know.

She glanced at the five-year-old bundle of curiosity seated beside her. Like his siblings, he wore a lightweight jacket, cotton pants and running shoes, all of which had clearly gotten some good use. "Actually, it was named after a horse."

"A horse!" the three older children said in the same breath.

Amanda nodded. "Jester was a wild horse that none of the men in the area could tame. But a woman by the name of Caroline Peterson managed to do it, much to their surprise, and a bronze statue of her and her horse was eventually commissioned and placed on the front lawn at Town Hall." Neglect due to faltering government finances had turned that same statue a mottled green in recent years, Amanda remembered, until the lottery win had given a much-needed boost to the local economy.

Now the tribute to woman and horse had been restored to its former shining glory, and several other improvements had been made around town—although more still could be done, Amanda had to concede. She just wished Jester's mayor wasn't proposing to change the whole character of a place far closer to small-town quaint than big-city progressive by turning it into a tourist attraction on a grand scale. Yes, it would bring even more money into the economy. But at what cost?

"Horseee!" Betsy suddenly shouted out. "Me see?"

"You will, honey," Amanda replied, flicking a look in the rearview mirror. She was pleased to find the little curly-haired blonde grinning from ear-to-ear. It heartened her, even though the rest of the children had barely cracked a smile since she'd picked them up at Family Services. She sensed their excitement, but there was wariness there, as well, especially on Liza's part. The eldest of the Bradley bunch clearly had a wait-and-see attitude.

"There's not much of Jester," she told them, "but I promise to show all of you around once we get you settled in."

"Will the husband you told us about be at our new home?" Again the question came from Caleb.

"Yes." She and the man of the house had agreed that she would pick the children up and spend a little time with them first before she introduced them to him. "He's anxious to meet you." And he was, she knew. She might have even contended that he was a bit nervous, judging by the way he'd been tapping a long finger on the breakfast table that morning while they'd discussed their game plan for the day, but she simply couldn't imagine Dev Devlin being nervous about anything.

As to her own nerves, they'd calmed at the sight of the four pairs of brown eyes she'd found waiting for her in Pine Run. Nothing could have reminded her more that her sisters and brothers were depending on her, and she wouldn't let them down. Even another set of eyes, the sharp hazel ones belonging to Louise Pearson, hadn't rattled her too badly as the social worker made no bones about the fact that she'd be keeping tabs on the Bradley case—close tabs.

They weren't out of the woods, that was plain. Not yet.

"Here we are," Amanda said as she pulled into a wide driveway minutes later. She could only be glad it was another sunny day. The house looked even more sparkling new, and somehow friendlier for that fact, than when thick spring clouds hid the wide sky above.

Dev appeared in the front doorway while she was

helping the children out of their seat belts. He must, Amanda thought, have been watching from one of the front windows. Windows that, like most of those on both floors of the house, now sported the drapes she'd chosen. She wasn't sure how she'd wound up as interior decorator, but somehow it had happened.

"Hi," he called. His long legs, clad in his usual Levi's, made quick strides toward the minivan.

Amanda no sooner set Betsy down than she toddled forward, heading straight for him. "Hi!"

A wide smile curved his mouth as she reached him. "You must be Betsy."

The little girl nodded and raised her arms. "Up!"

He glanced at Amanda. "Does that mean she wants me to…"

"Pick her up?" she finished at his hesitation. "That would be my guess."

Dev sucked in a breath. He wasn't about to admit that he'd never held a small child who wasn't much more than a baby before. And how difficult could it be? he asked himself. *Yeah, just be glad she's not demanding a diaper change, Devlin.*

He swallowed, hard. Then, reaching down, he caught her around the waist and lifted her into his arms. As light as a feather, that was how she seemed to him. Still, there was a soft yet sturdy feel to her, as well. As a test, he gave her a small bounce and was rewarded with a thin squeal, one of obvious enjoyment. It had him smiling again in no time.

Amanda introduced the rest of the children. They all stared back at him, eyes wide. "This is my husband, William Devlin," she said, completing the business.

The younger boy stood his ground as Dev walked

forward and extended his right hand. "Pleased to meet you, Patrick. You can call me Dev."

After a second the boy placed his palm in a far larger one and a brief handshake followed. Repeating the process with the other two children, Dev kept his smile in place. No one returned it, but that didn't bother him too much. At least they didn't seem to be afraid of him, even though he was bigger by leaps and bounds.

"Your rooms are all ready for you," he told the kids as they walked to the front door as a group.

"Mandy said we each get to have our own," Caleb said.

Mandy? Dev glanced at his wife. "Well, if…Mandy says so, you can believe it."

Liza, who'd been mostly silent so far, spoke up at that point. "Maybe Betsy and I should stay together."

"She'll be right across the hall from you," Amanda assured her. "And I'll keep a close eye on her, too, I promise."

Still holding Betsy, Dev joined Amanda in conducting a quick tour of the downstairs area. As they went from room to room, he didn't miss the way the three older children kept trading looks, as though they couldn't quite believe they'd landed in a place like this. It didn't surprise him, not taking into account the snapshot he'd seen of them with those few presents scattered around a Christmas tree. He'd been forced more than once while he was growing up to do without a tree or so much as a single present, and maybe that's why he'd given in to the urge to go all out when it came to buying things for these kids.

He didn't regret it, either, not for a second.

They climbed the center stairs and were steps from

the top when Rufus poked his furry black head out to view the new arrivals. "Kit-kat!" Betsy offered in a joyful shout, and the cat took off in a heartbeat.

"That was Rufus. He's a little shy," Dev explained. He looked at Betsy, who was hopping up and down as best she could with the secure grip he had on her. "I guess you like, ah, 'kit-kats,' huh?"

"Me and Patrick like them, too," Caleb told him, "but Liza likes them best."

Dev turned and settled his gaze on the girl who was bringing up the rear. "Did you ever have a cat?"

She shook her head, sending her golden curls fluttering. "We couldn't have one because our mom was allergic to them."

While Betsy babbled softly, the other kids fell silent at that point, as though the reference to their mother had brought their orphan status home to them. Then Amanda rushed into the breech, her voice staunchly upbeat. "Why don't you look at your rooms and we'll see what you think." She pointed to the left. "Yours is over there, Caleb. And yours is across from his, Patrick."

"We'll take Betsy to see her room while you guys check them out," Dev told the boys. When they took off, obviously curious, he headed in the opposite direction with Amanda and Liza at his side.

"That's your room, Liza," Amanda said with a short gesture as they approached another doorway.

Liza hesitated, then left them to investigate. Dev and Amanda walked into the smallest bedroom and quickly found themselves surrounded by a scene that featured sparkling white furniture paired with sunny yellow drapes and bright pictures of children's characters placed around the room.

"Big Bird!" Betsy declared, aiming an arm at a tall framed poster.

"Guess she likes *Sesame Street,* too," Dev murmured. Leaning over, he carefully set the pint-sized girl down on a colorful braid rug.

Amanda dropped to a crouch and placed a hand on a crib the shade of fresh snow on a Montana winter morning. "This is where you'll be sleeping, Betsy."

"And these," Dev said, striding over to a white wood chest decorated with more bright characters, "are some toys to keep you busy." With that, he opened the lid and watched sheer delight cross a chubby-cheeked face.

Dev trained his gaze on Amanda while Betsy rushed forward as fast as her tiny legs would carry her and dug into the chest. "Seems as though you knew what she'd like."

"But you're the one who insisted on buying so much." Amanda lifted an eyebrow. "Just don't forget it's my turn to have my way next."

He had to grin. "Looking forward to it…Mandy."

That earned him a fast frown. "As their big sister, I asked the children to call me that."

"Uh-huh."

"And I meant *only* the children," she added in a brisk tone as she straightened.

"Got it."

He crossed his arms over the front of his denim shirt, thinking that even when she was frowning up a storm at him he had a difficult time seeing her as the formidable female he'd locked horns with on a regular basis. It didn't seem to make a difference that she hadn't lost the habit of dressing for success, either. Today she had on another of her tailored outfits, this time a honey-colored pantsuit, but the soft glow he'd spied in her eyes every time she'd looked at the kids was a long way from businesslike. He had a hunch that remembering that sight would make it even harder for him to keep his hands off her. And it was getting plenty hard, already.

Trouble was, he kept wondering whether that wedding kiss was just an accident. Maybe if he kissed her again, he wouldn't be ready to gobble her up whole. Maybe he'd wind up concluding that it wasn't even much to write home about. Maybe.

"Holy cow!" Caleb said as he raced in from the hall, his eyes as round as saucers. "My room's got all kinds of things in it. Is that stuff really mine?"

Dev brought himself back to the matter at hand. "It sure is. And that goes for you, too," he told Patrick, who was one step behind his brother.

"I can't believe it," Liza murmured, walking in with a dazed expression. "My room is like a fairy tale, all blue and silver, and there's a dollhouse that looks like a castle."

"I've got a train set," Caleb told her, awe underscoring every word. "A big one."

"And I got a whole ranch, with animals and everything," Patrick chimed in, jumping up and down.

Betsy joined him with a plump teddy bear held in her tiny arms. "Yippee!"

Dev met Amanda's gaze over the heads of the children. "It's all yours, kids. Your big sister and I wouldn't have it any other way."

"Holy cow!" Caleb managed to get out one more time.

THAT EVENING, Dev arrived back home a little after ten o'clock. And *home* was the word that described the place, he decided, aiming an assessing look around him. A real home with some genuine warmth—and style, too, with small pillows in a leafy print to match the new living room drapes scattered about and a large rug the color of late-spring grass stretched across most of the floor. It was as if the outdoors had been brought inside. He damn sure would never have hit on the idea of doing anything like it, but he had to admire the results.

Having a wife, he thought, had its advantages.

He tipped his head back and glanced up the center staircase, wondering whether Amanda had gone to bed. Probably, he told himself. It was bound to have been a long day for her, what with getting the kids settled and all. As for him, he was looking forward to opening a beer and kicking back by the fireplace in the family room off the kitchen. Despite the abundance of liquid refreshment served at the Heartbreaker, he seldom drank anything more potent than club soda at the saloon. That was business, as far as he was concerned. Still, he enjoyed relaxing with a good brew when his day was done.

With that in mind, he started for the small bar the contractor had built next to the sliding doors leading to the rear deck. He'd nearly made it to the back of the house when he saw a light on in the normally dark family room. His usual habit was to turn on the wide-screen TV there and see if there were any late-night movies he wanted to watch. But no sound from the TV reached him now. Instead the stereo tuned to an easy-listening station filled the air with a deep voice singing a soft ballad. It wasn't the country-western he favored. No, it was far more likely, he figured, to be Amanda's choice in music.

Turning a corner, he saw her seated on the sofa. Here, as in the living room, she'd brought the outdoors inside with tailored drapes and scattered pillows, this time in a floral print. But it was the long, belted robe she wore that captured his attention in a heartbeat. Its shiny, clinging fabric was close enough to dusky rose to stir memories of the book cover he'd gotten a glimpse of the night he'd traded blows with a drunk before walking Amanda home. That novel, he had no trouble recalling, had *passion* as part of its title. He had to count himself lucky that it wasn't the book she had her nose in tonight. His wife was looking way too tempting as it was.

"Hi, there," he said, keeping his tone mild.

Obviously startled, she flashed a glance up at him. "You're home early." She hesitated. "I meant, aren't you usually at the saloon at least until midnight?"

He nodded. "That's been the case, yeah. Without the third bartender I just hired," he explained, "I'd have to be there when things got busy to take up any slack. Now I have more options, and tonight I got to thinking that it wouldn't hurt to start coming home sooner."

She shut her book. "It's your choice, but don't feel that because I'm changing my schedule with the children to consider, you have to change yours. The book-store doesn't do that much business between four and six anyway, and by closing it two hours earlier, we can eat dinner at a more reasonable time."

Dev tried not to dwell on the notion that she might prefer he didn't come home before midnight. "Well, whenever we eat, Caleb won't complain if carrots aren't on the menu," he said, referring to the fact that the five-year-old had expressed clear misgivings about anything in the vegetable department when they'd all sat down for their first dinner together that evening.

She lifted a brow. "He ate them, though, didn't he?"

He ran his tongue around his teeth. "That's because you can be a tough big sister when you need to be."

"Hmm. After you left, Patrick wasn't too thrilled, either, to learn that I expected him to take a bath every night and do a good job of washing behind his ears."

That had him grinning. "Sorry I missed the show. They sure were all smiling up a storm when Mabel brought over more brownies for dessert."

"All except Liza," she reminded him with a fleeting frown.

"True enough." Although the oldest Bradley kid had been quietly polite, even the grandmotherly Mabel hadn't been able to win herself more than the slightest of smiles from the girl.

"I've been doing my best not to worry about her," Amanda said with a short sigh.

"No reason you should yet," he replied. "Now, I'm going to get myself a beer. You want something?"

She shook her head. "No thanks."

"Okay. Be right back."

Amanda stared after him as he left the room, thinking that she could hardly head upstairs before he returned. Not that she didn't want to, but she simply couldn't be that rude, even if she'd never expected him to start coming home earlier. Certainly if she'd had any inkling, she wouldn't be sitting down here dressed for bed. While her robe covered her decently enough, she supposed, somehow that was little comfort.

Well, you'll just have to be sociable for a while, she told herself.

With that in mind, she set the mystery she'd been reading down on the end table next to the sofa and listened to another soulful ballad. It wasn't the best choice of music, she realized. Somehow it made the setting seem…intimate. And anything intimate was something she could have done without at the moment.

By the time Dev returned, he'd rolled up his shirt-sleeves to reveal strong forearms dotted with small swirls of crisp hair—another sight she could have done without, since it only emphasized the differences between them. Male. Female. Man. Woman. Not good.

"Feel free to turn on the television," she said.

"Actually, the music's not bad."

He walked over to the fireplace and set his bottle down on the mantel. It didn't take him long to have flames leaping to cast a soft glow over the room. That project completed, he settled into a tan leather recliner and took a long swallow of his beer.

"Maybe it will be easier for Liza to cope with all the changes once I get her started at Jester Public School tomorrow," she offered by way of conversation. "At least it will give her the chance to make friends with some second-graders in her age group."

"That could be a plus," he agreed. "Caleb's old enough to go to kindergarten, too, right?"

"Yes. After you went back to the Heartbreaker tonight, Mabel and I came up with a plan. Once breakfast is over and she gets here in the mornings, I'll walk Liza and Caleb to school before I open the Ex-Libris. Mabel will fix lunch for Patrick and Betsy and take them with her to pick up Caleb and Liza in the afternoons, then she'll head home when I get back.''

He dipped his head in a nod. ''Sounds like it'll work.''

''Then I'll have plenty of time to make dinner. Will it be okay with you if we eat around six o'clock most days? I'd like to get the children on a regular schedule.''

''No problem,'' he assured her. ''I'll be here.''

''And Sundays, when both our businesses are closed, would be the perfect time for you to make something on the grill.''

One corner of his mouth slid up. ''Didn't forget about that, did you?''

''Not on your life. I'd say we could go out to eat, too, but nothing much in Jester is open on Sundays and I'd rather not take the children back to Pine Run right now.''

''Too many memories,'' he summed up.

''Yes.''

''Okay, I'll step up to the plate and burn something on the grill.''

Amanda crossed one leg over the other. After making sure her robe was firmly closed, she swung a foot clad in a matching satin slipper. ''You're being good about this. And I have to say thank you.'' She could hardly say anything else, she recognized. Heaven only knew where her sisters and brothers would be at this moment if it weren't for Dev Devlin. Certainly they wouldn't be safely sleeping in their beds upstairs.

''No thanks necessary,'' he told her. ''Although,'' he added as his eyes met hers across the room, ''there is something, ah, in particular you could do for me…provided you're so inclined.''

Something she could do for him? Amanda brought her foot to a quick halt. Vivid visions of two tangled bodies danced in her head for a second before she wiped them out. If that's what he had in mind, she was by no means so inclined. Or at least most of her wasn't. If she wanted to be strictly honest with herself, she had to concede to feeling the pull of this man's gaze as it remained locked on her.

"And what would that be?" she asked at last in a cautious tone.

"You could classy up the Heartbreaker."

Amanda blinked. Whatever she'd been expecting, it certainly wasn't that. "What do you mean by 'classy up'?"

He shrugged. "Make it a place that might hold more appeal to a wider range of customers, I guess. I've been tinkering with the idea of sprucing up the saloon for a while, and now that I've moved out of the room behind the bar, I thought that maybe I could set it up as a spot to fix enough food so I could serve a few things along with the usual drinks."

She mulled that over for a moment. "I imagine, if you're serious about this, you could section off a separate dining area from the main room where people could eat."

"Yeah, that was my take on it, too. But I'm a long way from certain on how to make the whole thing look good. And since you did such a bang-up job here…"

Her eyes narrowed as he left that sentence hanging. "Now that you mention it, I'm not really sure how I wound up doing anything."

He lifted a shoulder in another shrug, suddenly looking a little too pleased with himself. "However it happened, you can't argue with success. All I'm asking is that you take a look at the bar and offer some suggestions.''

Why did she have the feeling that if she agreed, she'd be up to her ears in another decorating project? Then again, how could she turn him down when he'd already done so much for her and her family?

''All right,'' she said, ''I'll take a look at it.''

And that was her cue to leave, she thought, before she found herself agreeing to do who knows what. She retrieved her book and rose to her feet. ''I'm heading upstairs.''

Then, because something told her that her reluctant concession had him even more pleased with himself, she added, ''By the way, I don't think your feline friend will be sharing your room tonight.''

That statement put a puzzled frown on his forehead. ''What you do mean?''

She couldn't help but be glad she'd thrown him off balance, at least a bit. ''Rufus and Liza took a liking to each other when he finally ventured out for another look at the children. In fact, he followed her right into her room when the kids retired for the night and curled up at the foot of her bed.''

Dev shook his head. ''Deserted by a cat for a pretty face.'' He put his bottle down and got up to poke at the fire, sending banked flames leaping again. ''And now I have to sleep alone.''

''It won't hurt you,'' Amanda informed him, beginning to enjoy herself.

''Humph.''

''You sound like a boy who lost his favorite toy and needs a kiss to make it all better.'' The words were out before she realized how they could be taken. And how he indeed took them, she saw by the way he gradually straightened to his full height and looked at her.

"You may be on to something there," he murmured after a long moment. He hesitated for another second, then started toward her with measured steps.

"I was only joking," she hastened to assure him.

But he kept coming, and her pride wouldn't let her step back. She'd stood up to him too many times to turn and take off like a startled rabbit now. So she remained where she was, even when he closed the final gap, until there was nothing between them but the book she held clasped to her breasts. They both knew what was about to happen. She saw it in his eyes, those blue eyes that had taken on a determined gleam.

"This is a bad idea," she managed to get out as he lowered his head.

"Probably," he agreed.

Then he was kissing her, slowly and thoroughly, and before long she was kissing him back. *Not good...not good.* The words repeated in her mind even as other parts of her, suddenly needy parts of her, rose to silence them. How can anything that feels so good not be good? they asked. Caught between reason on one side and need on the other, she let need have its way.

But not for long, she promised herself as large hands—her husband's hands—caught her around the hips and gently pressed her closer, then closer still, until their lower bodies were all but fused together, reminding her in no uncertain terms of another vital difference between them. And all the while they kept on kissing each other as though there were no tomorrow, or yesterday. No future to concern them, and no past to rehash. Only now.

Only pleasure to take, and give. Only soft moans to join with low groans as tongues met and mouths slanted for a better fit. Only him. Only her. As if no one else in the world existed...only them.

Amanda wasn't sure who ended it first. One second their lips were locked, and the next they were standing stock-still and staring while their breaths came fast and hard. In the background, Rod Stewart sang about tonight being the night in his throaty voice, but she didn't believe that for a minute. Making tonight *the* night would be beyond foolish, she knew, now that her more practical parts were reasserting themselves.

The man still clutching her to him might have seen that in her gaze. Either that or he was speaking for himself when he released her and said in his own suddenly husky voice, "You're right, it was a bad idea."

Amanda swallowed, sure she could hear her heart continuing to hammer in her chest. "Yes, well, I'll see you tomorrow morning," she said in as calm a tone as she could muster. And with that, she finally whirled around and left the room.

It was Dev's turn to look after her as she departed. And to think about how her gently curved hips, covered only by a length of silky fabric, had felt under his rough-skinned palms. He was going to have one hell of a time forgetting it, he knew.

And he had to forget it. He'd never get a wink of sleep if he didn't. Before he'd seen that silent *no* forming in her eyes, forces below his belt had almost had him pulling her down to the rug where he could take things to their natural conclusion. Right now, his hormones were still so riled up, they were bound to take a while to settle down. Even a cold shower wouldn't do the trick, he more than suspected.

Blowing out a gust of air, he sprawled on the recliner and picked up his bottle for another long swallow. *Get a grip, Devlin,* he ordered himself as the cold liquid flowed down his too-tight throat. There was no point in thinking about what would have happened— what would be happening right this minute—if she'd said *yes*. No point at all.

And for all his current frustration, he reflected, he now had the answer to something he'd been wondering about since not long after he'd been pronounced a husband. That earlier kiss in the judge's chambers had been no accident. For a second time, after just one taste he'd been ready to gobble her up. For a second time, her soft-skinned mouth had proved to pack a potent punch. And maybe *this* time, it wasn't just basic hormones in action, either.

Hell, why deny it? He was actually getting to like Amanda Bradley Devlin.

Watching her with the kids was at least a part of it, he had to figure. After just one day, he had little doubt that she'd succeed in the role of substitute mother. She'd obviously taken to it like a duck to water.

He also had few doubts about the fact that she didn't see him as a substitute father. That seemed plain enough by the way she'd joined forces with Mabel to put together a schedule that left him by and large free of day-to-day responsibility for the kids. According to her, he'd didn't have to change his own schedule a bit.

So why had he decided to make some changes at the Heartbreaker in order to give himself more options? He didn't have to hire another bartender, but he had…because, dammit, he did want to come home sooner now that he had what he'd never had before—a place he could look forward to coming home to.

Dev lifted a hand and raked it through his hair. All right, so he didn't know much about being a parent—a good one, at any rate. Certainly Jed and Gloria Devlin had never provided a prime example of parenthood for him or his brother, Jed Jr., to follow. No one who'd been around in Jester while they were growing up would probably argue on that score.

"Cripes, it was just the opposite," he muttered to himself, remembering times when the young boy he'd been had wished he was anywhere but where he was, stuck with two people who didn't even seem to care a great deal about themselves, considering the way they were actually content to live in a ramshackle place, much less about their kids.

But, for all the things he'd never learned about being a father, a *real* father, Dev knew down deep in his gut that his determination to keep the four children now sleeping under his roof safe had only been reinforced by meeting them today.

"As long as they're under my protection, I'll do my best by them," he vowed, staring into the slowly fading flames across the room.

And, though it was as clear as the cloudless skies in some of the high mountain and lush meadow scenes now decorating the walls around his house that Amanda considered herself one self-sufficient person, he'd protect his wife, too.

That last thought had a smile tugging at his lips despite the fact that his body was still churned up enough to practically guarantee him some tossing and turning. Lord knows, the woman he'd married could be stubborn. But so could he.

If she needed any help from him, he'd see she got it—whether she liked it or not.

Chapter Seven

Amanda woke up to the sound of a small voice babbling a string of words, most of which she couldn't make out. Maybe because sleep had eluded her much too long the night before, she mused as she burrowed her head into the pillow. Her brain was still fuzzy.

Even so, she had little trouble recalling what had kept her awake. No, it would be far harder to forget last night's kiss, and most especially how she'd participated to the hilt in that enthusiastic meetings of mouths. Oh, yes, she had.

She knew it. And *he* knew it.

There was no getting around the truth of what had happened, and it might be wildly optimistic to so much as imagine she would be able to wipe out all traces of the memory of that kiss. Still, she could only conclude that it would be wise to try to put it behind her and go on from here. As both parties had agreed, it had been a bad idea and—

"Mandeee!" With that soft shout, the small voice in the background made itself known in no uncertain terms.

It was her wake-up call, Amanda realized as her eyes popped open. Even with the emerald brocade drapes she'd chosen for the master bedroom closed, thin rays of light filtered through. A glance at the clock on the pine nightstand confirmed that dawn had already put in an appearance. A few more minutes and the alarm would have gone off.

Amanda stifled a yawn as she got up, sending the hem of her long satin nightgown tumbling to her ankles. She shrugged into the matching robe, belted it, and walked across the room to open the side door she'd left partly ajar in order to keep an ear out for Betsy. It wouldn't have come as much of a surprise if the little girl had had problems sleeping in a new environment. As it had turned out, though, Betsy had enjoyed a far more restful night than her big sister.

"Mandeee!" Betsy called again from where she stood at the side of her crib, her tiny eyes widening at the sight of Amanda. "Up!"

"Good morning to you, too." Amanda found herself smiling despite the lack of sleep. She did as the little girl had commanded and hoisted Betsy into her arms. Nuzzling her nose in a riot of blond curls, she carried her burden over to the padded-top dresser. "Let's deal with your diaper, honey. Then we'll get some breakfast."

Betsy smacked her little lips.

"Okay, I get the message. You're hungry."

Fortunately Mabel, with thousands of diaper changes behind her, had offered to demonstrate how to get the job done with minimum trouble. Amanda had fumbled a bit on her first few tries the day before, but this morning all went well, and the row of snaps on the legs of Betsy's stretchy pink pajamas were soon refastened.

"A thousand more diapers and I may be as quick

as Mabel,'' Amanda told her companion. ''Want to take a toy with you downstairs?'' Goodness knows, she thought, there were plenty to choose from.

''Ted-bear,'' Betsy decided with a grin that seemed to come naturally to her sunny nature.

And so, after poking her head into three doors as she made her way down the hall to tell the other children that breakfast would soon be served, Amanda headed down to the kitchen carrying both Betsy and a fluffy brown teddy bear with beady dark eyes and a red felt tongue.

She'd learned at dinner the evening before that Betsy did a fairly good job of eating on her own, and by the time the rest of the pajama-clad children trooped in and took their places at the table, the littlest Bradley was perched in a snowy white high chair, making inroads on a bowl of warm cereal. Her small spoon held in one fist, she managed not to drop too much of her breakfast on its journey from bowl to mouth while the bear wedged in beside her looked on.

''Can we have pancakes?'' Caleb wanted to know.

''We like pancakes,'' Patrick explained with a hopeful expression.

''Me, too,'' a low voice added from the doorway to the hall.

Amanda glanced over her shoulder. As she'd expected, the man of the house was wearing a T-shirt and jeans, which seemed to be his usual morning attire. Unfortunately, rather than sticking to her habit of dressing before coming downstairs, she'd been too occupied with Betsy to take the time—something that wouldn't happen again, she promised herself, because she was getting up even earlier, starting tomorrow. The last thing she needed was to face Dev Devlin over the breakfast table wearing her robe—not to mention that it was the same robe his large hands had clutched to hold her tight to him just hours ago.

She cleared her throat. "All right," she said, "I suppose I can whip up a quick batch."

The boys were all smiles at that news. Noting that the eldest Bradley child didn't join in, Amanda asked, "Do you like pancakes, Liza?"

"Uh-huh," was her only reply. It looked as though she might be as quiet at breakfast as she'd been at last night's dinner.

"I'm glad to hear that," Dev said mildly as he walked over to the refrigerator and pulled out a can of coffee. "Because if you gals got together and decided you wanted something else, we guys would probably be out of luck."

"Girls get their way a lot," Patrick chimed in with a wise nod, suddenly looking older than his four years. "They can even be cowgirls and live on a ranch and *everything,* if they want to. That's what Mandy said, Mister—"

Shaking his head, Dev cut in smoothly. "I meant what I told you yesterday, kids. My last name is Devlin, but most folks in Jester call me Dev."

"Def," Betsy said, trying out the word.

"You almost got it right, honey." Amanda retrieved a paper towel and wiped dabs of stray cereal off the little girl's rosy cheeks. "It's Dev, with a *v.*"

Betsy mulled that over for a second, then declared "Deveee!" with a short pound of her spoon on the highchair's tray.

"No, it's just—" Dev started to say.

"Deveee!" Betsy repeated in no uncertain terms, looking as pleased as punch with her achievement.

Man and child exchanged a long look. "You know, for a pint-size person," he said at last, "I've got a hunch you can be as downright hardheaded as—" he switched his gaze to Amanda "—someone else in your family."

Liza finally spoke up. "Betsy's very smart," she told him in an earnest tone, defending her younger sister.

"I'll bet she is," he conceded.

"Just like," Amanda added with a proud lift of her chin, "the rest of the Bradleys."

He aimed a glance around the table. "Seems as though I'm outnumbered."

"You may well have met your match," Amanda agreed, noting that the three older children had followed her example and raised their chins a notch. She wanted to hug them. After all they'd been through, they still had spunk.

"Okay, I know when I'm licked," Dev grumbled. Despite his grousing, however, his lips twitched as he headed for the state-of-the-art coffeemaker on the counter. "I'll just do my job and wait for pancakes."

Then Betsy got the last word as she turned her empty cereal bowl over and plunked it on the teddy bear's head. "All done, Deveee!"

HE'D NEVER LIVE IT DOWN if it got out. Dev had been sure on that score ever since he'd found himself saddled with a new take on his name. Too bad he hadn't made much headway during the past few days on changing Betsy's mind about the whole thing, he thought on a windy morning that had clouds zipping past in the sky high over Main Street.

At least he'd been successful in getting Betsy's big

sister to take a break from her bookstore duties long enough to have a look around the Heartbreaker Saloon before it opened at noon. So far, she hadn't said a word as she'd walked around the place with a narrowed gaze.

"She's not planning on changing too many things, is she?" Roy asked in a low murmur, leaning over the bar.

Dev propped himself up on a stool and studied his head bartender. "Just a couple of improvements."

A wary frown creased Roy's weathered brow. "Would that be the female kind of improvements?"

"I suppose so," Dev allowed, letting his gaze drift back to his wife. "She's a female, all right." *And she damn sure feels like one when you've got your hands on her.* He didn't voice that thought yet couldn't deny how true it was. For days, he'd been trying not to remember how she'd felt. And mostly failing. Then, too, it didn't seem to matter anymore if she wore one of her dressed-for-business outfits. He had no trouble recalling how she'd looked in something soft and clinging.

None of it was doing him any good, he knew. He'd be a lot better off keeping his mind on the Heartbreaker and what he hoped to achieve here with Amanda's help.

"Even a doggone determined woman probably couldn't fancy this old place up too much," Roy said. The confirmed bachelor hesitated a beat, then added, "Could she?"

Dev ran his tongue around his teeth. With the saloon's long history as a rough-and-tumble spot reflected almost everywhere a person looked—from the scarred oak tables and mismatched chairs that had sur-

vived more than one brawl in earlier days to a corner
brass spittoon that just might qualify as a genuine antique—it was hard to figure that less than a miracle
would turn the Heartbreaker into anything close to a
showplace. Then again, Dev doubted that a determined
woman had ever taken on the challenge.

"I guess," he told Roy, "that remains to be seen."

The bartender snorted. Glasses clinked as he stacked
them on the long counter behind the bar. "I was afraid
you were going to say that." He kept his voice low
as Amanda, having completed her inspection, approached them.

"Well, what's the verdict?" Dev asked.

She took the stool next to his. "It has possibilities."

"Oh, Lordy," Roy muttered just loud enough to
make out.

Amanda slid him a sidelong glance. "Did you say
something?"

The bartender shook his head in a rapid motion,
sending his gray braids bobbing. "Nothing much."

Dev had to swallow a chuckle. "So, what possibilities are we talking about?"

She gestured toward a far corner of the large, high-
ceilinged room. "I think you could turn that space into
a separate seating area by putting up a half wall—
maybe one made of latticed wood to give it a more
open appearance."

"Sounds reasonable," Dev agreed after a moment's
consideration. "It would be convenient for serving
food, once the back room's converted to a full-blown
kitchen."

"Yes." She braced an elbow on the bar, her finely
knit sage-green sweater a sharp contrast to coarse
wood dulled by age. "You'll need some new chairs

to really make the seating area look good, but a few of the round tables you have now could be used if they were covered up with something. Chintz table-cloths might strike the right note.''

The two men's eyes met for a instant before Roy beat Dev to the punch. ''What's chintz?''

A knowing smile played around her lips, as if the question hadn't surprised her. ''It's a lightweight fabric made of glazed cotton.''

''Cotton,'' the older man repeated, suddenly looking hopeful. ''Nothing too fancy about that.''

''Well,'' Amanda said, ''it's not Irish linen, but I believe it will do the job.'' She paused. ''It wouldn't hurt to have some candles on the tables, too.''

Roy just stared at her, as if he couldn't begin to wrap his thoughts around the notion of candlelight flickering away—not in a place where boot-stomping music frequently flowed from the jukebox and trading jokes hardly fit for elegant drawing rooms was almost a tradition.

''I don't mean anything as elaborate as candelabras,'' she explained, clearly noting that she'd rendered the bartender speechless. ''I had something more along the lines of metal, lantern-style candleholders with a rustic finish in mind. They would have to be small enough to leave plenty of room for other things, of course. Have you decided on what you're going to serve?'' she asked Dev.

''I'm still mulling it over.'' Which was true enough, he thought. The only firm decision he'd come to was to do his best to get his wife to help him make some choices in the food department. He didn't plan on mentioning that just yet, though. First things first, he told himself. He'd won her agreement to offer advice about sprucing up the Heartbreaker. Now he had to try to ease her around to actively participating in the improvements.

For the life of him, he couldn't picture himself picking out chintz. Jeez, he needed her.

In more ways than one, something told him. But he wasn't thinking about the other ways. It was bound to lead to more frustration, and he'd done enough tossing and turning and tearing up the sheets—alone. He had a business to consider, and he was concentrating on that if it took every once of willpower he had.

"Were those all the changes you had in mind?" he asked.

"Not exactly," she replied after a short hesitation. "If you really want to appeal to a wider range of customers, it seems to me you have to take into account that some people might not appreciate the more, ah, macho aspects of Western history on display here."

Dev crossed his arms over his chest, reminding himself that she hadn't called *him* macho. Not this time. No, she'd set her sights on something else.

"You don't mean the row of horseshoes nailed over the front door, do you?" Roy asked, sounding worried again. "It'd be bad luck to take them down, I'm thinking."

Amanda gave her head a slow shake. "No, not that."

"Humph. Well, I reckon the longhorns might give some folks pause," the bartender allowed, waving a hand toward the broadly curved cattle horns set high on a dark paneled wall, "but—"

"No, it's not that, either," she said, breaking in with another shake of her head.

Then what in tarnation is it? Dev could all but see that question forming in Roy's eyes.

As if she'd caught it, as well, Amanda scooted around on her stool and faced the rear of the bar. Switching her gaze back and forth, she studied the oil paintings hung at opposite sides of a wide mirror. Bordered by heavily carved gold frames, both works of art featured full-figured women wearing next to nothing, the first reclining on a length of lacy material and the second playing cards with a man—or maybe *customer* would be a better word—in the middle of an old-fashioned brass bed. No one knew for certain how long the pictures dating back to a lustier era had held prominent places at the saloon. One thing for sure, it was long enough for them to achieve legend status.

Roy looked at Dev. "Oh, Lordy," he muttered one more time. "I've got the feeling she means…"

As his voice drifted to a halt, Amanda dipped her chin in a brisk nod. "Yes," she said. "I do."

THE MERCANTILE, housed in one of the largest buildings on Main Street, was a modern-day version of a general store. From alphabet blocks to zodiac calendars, the Mercantile sold it all. It had clothing. It had housewares. It had office, pet and hobby supplies.

And it certainly had fabrics, Amanda thought as she headed toward the long counter at the rear of the store, where thick bolts of whatever suited a person's fancy could be unwound and measured out. It came as no surprise to find that she had to skirt around several other customers and the clerks helping them locate exactly what they needed on the many shelves and racks comfortably cluttering the place. Most everyone in Jester wound up shopping here. Only the small post office across the street probably saw more of the town's citizens on a regular basis.

What did turn out to be somewhat surprising, however, was the sight of Ruby Cade standing behind the counter. In the months since the slender redhead in her early thirties and the career air force man she'd married had shared in the lottery win, Ruby had bought the old Tanner farm, and now she seemed to spend a good deal of her time there. These days, it was more common to see her business partner and co-owner of the Mercantile, Honor Lassiter, presiding over the store.

Ruby's mouth curved in a faint smile as she took notice of her latest visitor. Amanda waved a greeting in return, thinking that the green-eyed woman with milky fair skin and a dab of freckles had once smiled widely. Strangely enough, that had been before the jackpot winners were announced during one of the frequent periods when Sam Cade was away on military duty. Winter had turned to spring, but Captain Cade was still away somewhere, and his wife was said to have filed for a divorce in his absence.

So much for money buying happiness, Amanda reflected to herself.

"How are you?" Ruby asked. "Honor's been telling me that the Devlins have become our best customers in recent weeks."

"I'm fine," Amanda replied, "and I suppose Honor must be right." Just the children's things alone had meant several trips to the store. Amanda could only be glad that her sisters and brothers had settled in and the schedule she and Mabel had set up was working well. Normally she'd be heading home after closing the Ex-Libris to take over from the doting nanny, but this afternoon she had an errand to do first—courtesy of her husband.

"I imagine it must have taken a lot to furnish that big new house," Ruby said, smoothing a hand down the front of the denim jumper she wore with a corn-flower blue blouse. "What can I help you with to-day?"

"I need some cotton chintz, several yards of it, that I'll be having made into tablecloths."

Ruby nodded. "I suppose a big house means plenty of dining space, as well."

"Actually, the tablecloths are for the Heart-breaker," Amanda explained.

One of Ruby's eyebrows winged up. "The Heart-breaker?"

"The *Heartbreaker*," a deep male voice said yet again from behind Amanda.

She turned to find Dean Kenning, decked out in his white barber's coat, standing a short step away. "As it happens," she told him, "I'm making a few im-provements at the saloon."

He stared her, his expression turning wary in a heartbeat. "Does Dev know about this?"

"He's the one responsible for my getting involved in the first place." Amanda knew that nothing could be more true. For a second time, her husband had won her agreement to help him without her being quite sure how he'd accomplished it. The man was devious, she thought. That had to be it.

Dean shook a head topped by a thatch of dark brown hair without a speck of gray in it. The barber not only cut his own hair, it was fairly plain that he dyed it as well. "Tablecloths at the Heartbreaker," he muttered. "Please don't tell me they're going to have flowers sprouting all over them."

Amanda thought about saying yes and wouldn't daffodils be wonderful just to see what how much pure horror that would produce on the big man's ruddy face. "No," she said instead, resisting temptation as she turned back to Ruby. "I'm thinking of something more in earth-tone shades."

"I may have just what you want," Ruby replied after a second's consideration.

In a matter of moments Amanda, with Dean at her side, was studying a subtle print featuring small squares of deep russet and creamy beige. "I'm glad you were here today," she told Ruby. "You may be spending a lot of time at the farm, but it's obvious that you're still on top of your merchandise. This is perfect."

Ruby smiled her faint smile. "Glad to be of service. I do like it at the farm, but the Mercantile is special, too."

"Got to wonder why she likes it so much out there," Dean said under his breath as Ruby called a clerk over to help measure and cut the fabric.

Amanda pretended not to hear that comment, even though she had little doubt as to what was going through the barber's mind. If she'd gotten wind of a few recent rumors about a tall, dark and definitely attractive man—a man who wasn't Ruby's air force officer husband—taking up residence at the Cade farm, Dean must have heard them, too. Local gossip thrived at the barbershop even more than it did over tea and pastries at the bookstore. Not that it was any of her—or anyone's—business, Amanda reminded herself.

Ruby rolled up the cut chintz and set it on the counter. "Anything else you need?"

"Yes. Some sheer ivory lace."

This time, both of the store owner's brows went up. "If it's for the Heartbreaker, I can't wait to hear what you intend to do with it."

Amanda had to grin, thinking that this was one task she would enjoy doing. "You know the paintings of the, shall we say, generously endowed women hanging in back of the bar?"

"Mmm-hmm," Ruby murmured.

"I plan to do some discreet draping and cover them up."

"Cover them up!" Dean repeated, sounding scandalized. "Those two gals are practically an institution in this part of Montana."

"Don't worry, you'll still be able to see them through the lace," Amanda informed him with a sidelong glance. "Just not in all their, ah, glory."

Dean looked like he wanted to groan in protest. Instead, he said, "I'd better head out. If I stick around, you're liable to tell me Dev's going to start playing Beethoven on the jukebox."

"What did you come in for?" Ruby asked before he could leave.

He blinked. "Land sakes, it went right out of my head with all the talk about tablecloths and lace. I popped over to spread the news that Luke McNeil just made an announcement. According to the sheriff, the park pavilion falling down last month was no accident."

No accident.

The words echoed in Amanda's mind. At least that puzzle had been solved, she thought, remembering how the picnic pavilion had collapsed without warning during Jester's Founders' Day celebration. Fortunately only one person had been injured, and that injury had proved not to be critical. But everyone knew it could have been much worse.

And now, as it turned out, someone had apparently done it on purpose—which, of course, only gave rise to more questions. Namely, who had done it? And why?

AMANDA CONTINUED to mull over the pavilion matter as she drove home with her purchases resting in the back of the minivan. She left Big Draw Drive and turned down Maple Street, still wondering what might possibly lead anyone to bring down a structure that had been a part of Jester for so long. Then, as she approached the house, the sight of a strange car in the Devlins' driveway had her considering another question entirely.

Who was their unexpected visitor?

She pulled up next to the blue sedan, switched off the engine and got out. Although far from new, she noted that the car seemed well maintained. And for the life of her she couldn't come up with a possible owner.

Not one of the recent millionaires, that was certain. Late-model luxury vehicles, once a rarity in Jester, had become a fairly common sight. Set against the backdrop of the old buildings lining Main Street, they offered a marked contrast. Tradition going back to pioneer days versus modern conveniences the rugged people who had first settled Jester would probably have gawked at with all the wide-eyed wonder a spaceship landing from outer space would produce during present times.

Amanda's mouth curved at the thought. It widened to a full-blown smile when she opened the front door and the smell of fresh baking greeted her. These days, Mabel not only used the oven at her own home to good effect but had also taken to filling the Devlin place with sweet and now familiar scents.

"You've worked your magic again, Mab—" Amanda started to say. Then her voice died right along with her smile at the sight of the two women seated in the living room.

One was Mabel, holding Betsy in her lap and looking even more like Mrs. Claus in a ruffled red apron.

The other was Louise Pearson, looking exactly like a no-nonsense government representative in an olive suit that couldn't have been more plain. It had *official* written all over it.

"Hello, dear," Mabel said brightly. "As you see, we have a visitor."

Amanda plastered another smile on her face, hoping it didn't look as forced as it felt. "Yes." She met the social worker's gaze across the room. "We weren't expecting you," she said as lightly as she could manage.

"No, you wouldn't be," Louise didn't hesitate to tell her. "Child and Family Services doesn't give any notice when it conducts an inspection. We've found that's the best way to learn the true state of things."

An inspection. A *unexpected* inspection. Well, they would just have to deal with it, Amanda told herself as she walked across the room and sat on the sofa next to Mabel.

"Mandeee!" Betsy cried in a bid for attention that

transformed to giggles when Amanda pulled the little girl into her lap and nuzzled her nose in the crease of a tiny neck.

"Did you have a good day, honey?" she asked, straightening.

Betsy's chin went up and down in a rapid nod. "Cookies," she replied, as if that explained it all.

"Mabel made some," Amanda summed up.

"And the children helped," Mabel added. She looked at Louise. "They're getting very good at cutting out the dough and putting sprinkles on top."

Seated across from the sofa in an overstuffed chair, Louise merely dipped her head in response.

While Betsy quietly clapped her hands and sang a garbled version of a *Sesame Street* song, Amanda leaned back and tried to relax. There was nothing to worry about, she assured her nerves, at least not as far as the children were concerned. Family Services would find that things were going as well as anyone could expect. Liza and Caleb had shown no reluctance to attend school, and Patrick and Betsy were undeniably content to spend their days with Mabel. When they were all together, Amanda had done her best to create a loving family atmosphere.

Not, of course, that everything went smoothly all the time. Caleb was inclined to try a slide down the staircase banister when he thought he could get away with it, and Patrick had to be regularly reminded to put his toys away. The children also had disagreements between themselves, although less than many siblings. Losing their parents at such a young age had clearly created even closer bonds than usual.

As far as dealing with the most recent change in their lives, only Liza obviously remained wary, as though she couldn't quite believe that there was no longer any need to be concerned about the future. Amanda longed to see one of the sunny grins Betsy so readily displayed on Liza's face. Somehow she knew that when that happened she could let go of her own concerns about the eldest Bradley child.

All in all, though, no one could say that her sisters and brothers were worse off for having come to Jester. Just the opposite, in fact. No, as far as this impromptu inspection was concerned, Amanda felt safe in concluding that only thing to possibly worry about was—

"When will your husband be home, Mrs. Devlin?" Louise asked.

Yes, that could well be the problem area. Amanda knew it by the way the social worker's gaze lit with a we'll-just-see-about-this gleam. It seemed that, although she'd consented to allowing the Bradley children to be placed in Amanda's care, Louise still had her doubts about the hasty marriage in Pine Run. Fortunately by now the bride and groom had gotten some practice at playing the role of happily wedded couple.

"Please call me Amanda," she said, her tone staunchly polite. "Dev will be home in plenty of time for dinner. We usually eat at six o'clock."

"They like to keep the children on a fairly fixed schedule," Mabel explained to Louise, "and I think it's best, don't you?"

"Yes, I believe it is." The gleam in the social worker's eye didn't dim a wait. "The dinner hour can also be an important time for children to benefit from parental influences. How the group interacts at mealtimes can be very…telling."

Amanda hesitated, then decided to take a risk. "You're more than welcome to join us," she said, and couldn't help but be pleased when the invitation seemed to startle Louise, at least for a moment.

"You should," Mabel told their visitor. "This is such a nice family. Ike and I are so glad to have them as neighbors. And as for the newlyweds—" eyes sparkling, she slid a sidelong glance at Amanda "—well, as I've said before, it's so wonderful to see young love in bloom."

A second of sheer silence followed that statement. Then, frowning thoughtfully, Louise said, "Since my husband is currently out of town on business, perhaps I will accept."

"Good." Amanda plastered another smile on her face and met the challenge. "We'll be happy to have you."

"But first," Louise told her, "I was waiting for you to return before I inspected the children's rooms and had a private word with the older ones."

Mabel rose to her feet and looked down at Amanda. "I'll be going, dear. Liza's upstairs doing her homework, and the boys are in the family room watching television." Leaning over, she patted one of Betsy's chubby legs. "I'll see you all tomorrow."

Betsy grinned. "Cookies?"

Mabel laughed. "I do believe she's going to become my best helper."

Amanda stood, still holding Betsy. "I think you'll find the children's rooms will pass muster," she told Louise.

Nodding, the social worker got up in one efficient motion. "It's merely a formality. My report has to state that they have certain necessities."

Amanda pursed her lips, thinking that the woman who conducted surprise visits could well wind up being surprised herself once she got a look at how many *necessities* the Bradley bunch had, including closets now filled with new clothes to replace the undeniably worn clothing they'd brought with them. And while a private talk with the children might unearth a few complaints about regular baths with thorough ear washings and vegetables that couldn't be ducked at mealtimes, Amanda was fairly sure all would go well there.

The real question was: Would today put an end to Louise's doubts about the Devlin marriage?

It wouldn't hurt, Amanda decided, to call her husband at the Heartbreaker and warn him that the happily wedded couple had another performance in store for them.

To satisfy one particularly eagle-eyed representative of Family Services, she knew it would have to be good.

Chapter Eight

"Sweetheart, I'm home!"

With those ringing words, Dev closed the front door behind him. After stowing his hat and jacket in the closet, he started toward the rear of the house, grateful that Amanda had given him a heads-up. He'd at least had the short walk from the saloon to prepare for the prospect of dealing with the formidable Mrs. Pearson. Too bad he'd already discovered that he was more likely to suddenly sprout wings than charm the social worker into anything with an easy grin.

He couldn't say it was a first, either. Any charm he might lay claim to had also seemed to be wasted on the hardheaded female he'd been denied so much as a glimpse of lately when he got back to the house after his second shift at the Heartbreaker. By ten o'clock, she'd been tucked away in her room.

Which was just as well, he told himself. Keeping his mind off the one occasion when they'd shared a late-night conversation—and a lot more—in front of a flickering fire was bound to be harder if they spent too much time alone.

"Hello, dear." His wife gave him a blinding smile

as she met him at the doorway to the family room.
"We have company."

Figuring their *company* could well be watching, he
bent and planted a brief kiss on her lips, knowing better than to linger over it. That would only get him into
trouble. "I saw a car in the driveway."

"Unfortunately *I* had no idea who it belonged to
when I saw it," Amanda told him in a hasty whisper
before raising her voice to add, "Family Services
stopped by to see how the children were doing." Summoning another smile, she took his arm and led him
into the room where four kids lounged on the plush
ivory rug in front of the TV while a large-boned
woman with graying hair scraped back in a bun sat,
spine straight, at the end of the sofa closest to the
doorway. "I'm sure you remember Louise Pearson."

I wouldn't be likely to forget her, Dev thought,
dredging up a slow grin despite being all but certain
that it wouldn't do him a lick of good. "Nice to see
you again," he told their visitor.

Predictably, the social worker merely narrowed her
gaze and dispensed with any small talk. "I wouldn't
have considered my report complete unless I saw you,
Mr. Devlin."

He didn't miss the meaningful edge to that statement. Even if Amanda hadn't warned him, he'd have
been pretty fast in concluding that their rushed wedding was still being questioned. "Then I'm glad you'll
be able to do a thorough job, Mrs. Pearson," he said,
keeping his tone mild.

"No need to stand on ceremony with each other,"
Amanda broke in, still holding on to her smile. By her
fingernails, Dev suspected. She couldn't have failed to

notice the undercurrents in that last exchange any more than he had.

"Louise is going to stay for dinner," she explained to her husband as if she were passing along that news for the first time. "Under the circumstances, she and I have already agreed that it would be more comfortable to be on a first-name basis."

"Sure thing," he replied as he switched his gaze back to the social worker. "Feel free to call me Dev."

"Deveee!" Betsy wasted no time in countering from her spot on the rug.

That did what the man once known for his wily ways with women had failed to do. It had Louise's straight-as-an-arrow lips curving at the tips as the pint-sized girl toddled over to him and raised her arms. "Up!"

"Yes, your little majesty." He lifted her in one smooth motion. "I live to serve."

"They get along so well together," Amanda cheerfully informed their guest.

"The kid has turned out to be as crazy about me as my wife is," Dev found himself contending as a small devil sparked to life inside him and urged him on. "In fact, neither of them can keep their hands off me."

"Is that so?" Louise asked, arching a brow.

"Absolutely," he replied.

While Amanda stood stock-still beside him, Betsy readily backed him up by tugging on one of his ears. He gave her a short bounce he knew by now was guaranteed to produce giggles. It took a few more bounces, and a lot more giggling, before she demanded, "Down!" and toddled back to join Liza and the boys.

"Well, dinner's almost ready," Amanda said, tucking her casual cream-colored top more firmly into the waistband of her tan slacks. "Want to help me get it on the table, dear?"

"Absolutely," Dev replied for a second time. "Will you excuse us…Louise?"

At the social worker's nod, Amanda added, "When this program is over in a few minutes, kids, you can go up and wash your hands. And make sure you take any toys you brought downstairs with you and put them away." The last comment was offered with a pointed glance at Patrick.

With that, the Devlins left the room and headed for the kitchen at a fast clip. Once they were safely out of hearing distance, Dev said, "Sorry you got blindsided by this. How has it gone so far?"

"As well as can be expected, I think." Amanda retrieved some pot holders from the counter and pulled a large casserole dish from the oven. "The children's rooms passed her inspection with flying colors, and she seemed satisfied after the private talk she had with them."

He rolled up the sleeves of his denim shirt. "Don't worry, we'll get through the rest of it. Some tasty food mixed with a helping of friendly conversation, plus a couple more *sweethearts* and *dears* tossed in for good measure, should get the job done."

She blew out a breath. "At least Mabel is on our side. She's so convinced of how happily wedded we are, she didn't hesitate to rave about it before she left."

"That can't have hurt," he allowed.

"I suppose not," Amanda agreed as she started for the dining room with the casserole in hand. But the thought that dogged her heels as she walked down the hall was that Mabel was one thing, and Louise another.

She set the heavy white dish at one end of the long pine table and cast a critical eye over the paisley place mats she'd chosen to compliment the new maroon drapes. With a small spray of fresh herbs acting as a centerpiece, the room looked comfortably homey, if she did say so herself. At the moment she could only be glad for the effort she'd put into decorating the house. No one, not even the most discriminating of people, could contend that the Devlin place wasn't a good spot to raise children.

It had to weigh in their favor when it came to filling out Louise's report. Now if they could just get through dinner without any stumbles on the path to winning the social worker over once and for all. No, if *she* could get through dinner, Amanda amended. Something told her that the man she'd married would have little trouble furthering a friendly, not to mention convincing, conversation.

By the time she was dishing out second helpings of baked chicken and creamy rice, that theory had proved to be true. Liza had been her usual quiet self, and the large black cat curled on the floor beside her only offered a purr now and then when she did her best to secretly drop a bite of something his way. But between Betsy's merry babbling, the two boys' cheerful bantering, and the man of the house's knack for playing the contented husband, all traces of the undercurrents evident in his earlier exchange with their unexpected company had disappeared.

Things were going well. Amazingly well, Amanda thought as her spirits took a definite turn for the better.

Before long dessert was finished and the older children were helping Dev clear everything off the table. For her part, Amanda could have slumped in her seat and looked heavenward in sheer gratitude, she was that relieved. Inviting Louise Pearson to join them for dinner had been the right decision. Somewhere along the way, the woman with the admirably straight spine had even relaxed enough to lean back in her chair.

''That was delicious,'' Louise said from her place at one side of the table. ''You're a good cook, Amanda.''

More than the words, the cordial tone in which they'd been issued was music to her hostess's ears. ''Thank you, Louise.''

''You and husband interact well with the children. And,'' Louise added after a short pause, ''you also seem to deal well with each other.''

If you only knew how much we once would have gone out of our way not to deal with each other. ''Living together has proved to be a, ah, stimulating experience,'' Amanda said with a wide smile, hoping she wasn't laying it on too thick. Not that it wasn't true that it had been stimulating, she reminded herself. Maybe too much so in some respects, because even though Dev Devlin had told an out-and-out whopper earlier by saying that she couldn't keep her hands off him, she knew she wouldn't be making sure she was upstairs before he came home for the night if the thought of her hands *on* him had no effect on her.

They should have both kept their hands—and lips— to themselves right from the day they'd stood before the judge and said ''I do.'' Of that, Amanda was certain.

''Do you have a restroom downstairs?'' Louise asked. ''I probably should use it before I head home.''

Amanda nodded. ''The quickest way is to go through the family room,'' she instructed. ''It's the door on the far side of the room, just past the television.''

''All done!'' Betsy announced as Louise left the dining room. With no teddy bear currently seated beside her, the little girl settled for scraping her spoon on the high chair's tray instead of dumping the bowl that had held her ice cream over the bear's head. ''Kit-kat!'' she added with a look down at Rufus. As though he had no intention of risking having something dumped on him, the cat took off.

Amanda stood and hoisted Betsy up. ''I'm glad you're eating good, honey, even if you are getting heavier every—''

A startled cry—a woman's cry—suddenly broke in, followed in a heartbeat by a loud thump.

It could only be Louise, Amanda thought as she gripped Betsy tighter and rushed out into the hall. Dev and the other children, coming from the kitchen, were a short step in front of her as they all raced into the family room. There, they found the social worker stretched out full length on the rug and staring wide-eyed at the ceiling.

''Oh, my God.'' Amanda quickly set Betsy down and knelt beside Louise. ''What happened?''

''I...I believe I slipped on something,'' was the older woman's breathless reply. ''My foot seemed to go right out from under me.''

''And I think I see why,'' Dev said in a sober tone.

Amanda looked up at him. ''What do you mean?''

He dipped his head toward an object resting on the floor inches away. It was a little ranch wagon, with a brown plastic body and shiny black wheels. "Seems to me I've seen that toy before."

"Mmm-hmm," Amanda murmured.

With that, four heads—Amanda's, Dev's, Liza's and Caleb's—turned in unison to gaze at Patrick. The four-year-old shuffled his feet, swallowed hard and finally managed to get out one short and very quiet statement.

"Uh-oh."

UH-OH. Yeah, that about summed it up, Dev thought as Amanda shooed the kids upstairs and footsteps faded away. Invite someone to stay for dinner, someone who had the power to file a report that could grab you by the short hairs, and then send her sprawling right after dessert.

"Can you wiggle your fingers and toes?" he asked Louise. She was still stretched out on the floor, where he'd firmly suggested she remain until they had a better handle on any possible injuries.

"Yes," she replied after a second.

"Any pain anywhere?"

"Not at the moment."

Dev mulled the matter over for a minute. "Okay, maybe you should try sitting up." When she agreed, he slid an arm under her shoulders. As he slowly raised her upper body, he didn't miss the brief wince that crossed her face. She was hurt. Maybe not badly, but enough to have him frowning in a flash.

Amanda hurried back into the room, her expression solemn. "I'm so sorry, Louise."

Their visitor drew in what sounded like a steadying breath. "Unfortunately these things happen."

"It shouldn't have happened here," Dev muttered.

"You're right," Amanda wasted no time in agreeing. "Believe me, I intend to have another talk with Patrick about putting his things away. He doesn't know how seriously someone could be injured through carelessness."

Dev's frown deepened. "Maybe he'd understand better if he wasn't allowed to play with that particular toy for a day or two."

"Actually, that's an excellent idea," Louise told him, sitting straighter. "I wouldn't have thought it of a man who lived a bachelor's life for quite a while, but you seem to have a grasp on parenting. Then again, I've found that sometimes the last person one would expect to take on the role of family authority figure is a natural."

A natural? *Him?* Dev figured Louise's fall must have rattled her brain right along with the rest of her. If he had a talent for anything, it was running a saloon, not parenthood. "Want to try standing?" he asked, dropping the subject.

At her nod, he helped her up, but it took only a few steps to demonstrate that the social worker was hardly in top-notch condition. "Perhaps I'd better sit for a bit," she said, limping over to the sofa and carefully lowering herself down on a plump cushion. "I may have thrown my back out."

Amanda fluffed up a floral-print pillow and placed it behind Louise. "I think we should get a doctor to look at you."

Louise shook her head. "I don't believe that's necessary. For all that I'm an advocate of good posture and have practiced it for years, I've had this type of problem before. The best remedy seems to be rest.

With the help of my heating pad, I should be fine by tomorrow.''

Amanda didn't look convinced. "Even if that's the case, you probably shouldn't be trying to drive anywhere tonight.''

Louise hesitated. "You may have a point there," she reluctantly acknowledged.

"Well," Dev said after a second's consideration, "if Mabel will come over and watch the kids, Amanda and I can take you back to Pine Run. She can drive your car, and I'll follow in my Jeep so we'll have transportation back to Jester.''

Louise reclined against the pillow with another wince. "Or, rather than putting you to all that trouble, perhaps I could just spend the night here.''

Spend the night *here?* Dev slid a sidelong look at Amanda and found her eyes waiting to lock with his. It took less than a second for him tear his gaze away and say, "It'd be no trouble.''

"Certainly not," Amanda added.

But now Louise was the one who looked less than convinced by those hasty assurances. "A forty-mile drive round trip would hardly be convenient.''

He lifted one shoulder in an offhand shrug, deciding to take a more laid-back approach. The last thing he wanted to do was arouse any suspicion about the fact that having overnight company—especially company in the form of the person who still had that blasted report to file—could be a lot more than inconvenient. It could be downright risky.

"Nevertheless," Louise continued, looking straight at him, "I wouldn't have suggested an alternative solution if I hadn't recalled your mentioning a guest room.''

Had he? Cripes, he had, Dev had to admit. During the meeting with Family Services right after the wedding, he'd actually boasted about the new Devlin house having six bedrooms—including an extra one. At the time, he'd been set on making an impression. Now the bald truth that the room in question was actually the one he'd been sleeping in, and without so much as a cat for a bed companion lately, had come back to bite him.

Amanda cleared her throat. "Yes, the guest room." It was plain that she'd remembered the same conversation he had. Squaring her shoulders, she turned his way. "I suppose it wouldn't take long to get it ready for Louise."

He resisted the urge to blow out a gusty breath. "I guess not," he said in an even tone.

"How about if I make you a cup of tea?" she asked their visitor. "You can put your feet up and relax while we get things organized."

"That's very gracious of you," Louise said. "I appreciate your hospitality."

"No," Amanda replied with firm directness, "we're the ones who appreciate how good you're taking this. Hopefully by tomorrow you really will be fine."

With that, Amanda whipped around and headed for the kitchen at a fast clip. Dev wasted no time in following her out the door. She put a kettle on to boil before turning to face him as he stood with one hip propped against a counter. "Don't say I shouldn't have offered."

He crossed his arms over his chest. "I won't. I figured our backs were against the wall."

"How long do you think it will take to move your things?" she asked with an unreadable expression.

She wasn't questioning where they'd be moved to, he noticed. She obviously knew as well as he did that there was only one spot available, and that was the master bedroom.

The bedroom they'd be sharing tonight.

"I can throw the stuff in the bathroom and dresser into a couple of suitcases," he told her. "I'll leave what's in the closet."

She nodded. "I doubt Louise will go in there."

He blew out the gust of air he'd held back earlier. "If she does, we can just say that you have so many clothes, I had to keep mine down the hall."

Amanda's mouth took a wry slant. "Spoken like a true male, but I suppose it's as good an explanation as any." She paused. "You wouldn't happen to have a heating pad among your meager belongings, would you?"

"Nope. But I can make a quick run to Cozy's Drug Store. Doing whatever it takes to get our guest on her way in the morning works for me."

"Heaven knows, it works for me, too," she said as the kettle whistled. She quickly fixed the tea. "I'll meet you upstairs in a minute. I can put clean linens on the bed while you pack up."

"Sounds like a plan, but we're going to have to do this whole thing on the sly, you know. It wouldn't exactly be helpful if one of the kids mentioned over the breakfast table that they saw me hauling my suitcases around."

She blinked. "Good Lord, I never thought of that."

One corner of his mouth quirked up. "You obviously haven't had a lot of practice at being sneaky."

"No, I guess not," she allowed. "I suppose you'll have to show me how it's done."

"Be glad to."

He watched her head back to the family room, tea-cup in hand, thinking of some other things he could probably show her. Things that had nothing to do with being sneaky.

Things that he'd damn well better stop thinking about right now.

IN THE WHIRLWIND of activity that followed, Dev started packing as Amanda tidied the "guest" room, doing her best to make it look as unlived in as possible. It turned out to be a far easier task than she knew it would have been had their situations been reversed and she was the one moving her belongings. Besides his clothing and bathroom essentials, there was little of a personal nature to deal with. She couldn't help noting the lack of so much as one family photograph, where several of her and her mother dating back to happier days for both of them were scattered around her room. In all the time she and Dev Devlin had spent together since their marriage, he'd never mentioned his relatives, either, not after the brief conversation they'd had over dinner before the children arrived, during which he'd made it fairly plain that he had no desire to discuss his family.

Then again, she reminded herself, except for answering the children's understandable questions about the father they shared, she had little wish to discuss Sherman Bradley. Some things were better left alone. That was her feeling, and apparently her husband felt the same way.

"I think that will do it," Amanda said, leaning over to spread a white terry cloth robe across the navy comforter. Fortunately, she thought, the man of the house had been able to come up with a robe that looked as though it had seldom been used. The sturdily-built Louise, who'd never fit into anything the woman of the house could lend, would at least have something to wear for the night.

"Looks fine to me," Dev agreed with a brief glance around. "Why don't you take the kids downstairs to say good-night to our guest? I'll move my suitcases when the coast is clear."

She couldn't fault his strategy. "You're good at this sneaky stuff."

"I do my best," he told her dryly.

"Hmm. Well, I have to admit you can be handy to have around on occasion."

"Uh-huh." He met her gaze. "And by the way, I don't snore, either."

Just like that, what neither of them had acknowledged in so many words, was out.

They would be spending the night together.

Their choices, Amanda had already concluded, were few to none in that respect, not unless they wanted to chance putting one of the downstairs sofas to use as a makeshift bed. However slim the possibility, the fact remained that Louise wasn't so badly injured that she couldn't leave her room. There was always the chance that she might stumble on her host or hostess sleeping at a good distance from each other, and any illusion of a happy couple would go up in smoke.

"I'm relieved to hear you say so," she told him in a deliberately calm voice.

"Funny, you don't look all that relieved," he countered, his tone still as dry as dust. "In fact, you look like you could use a stiff drink."

She probably could, Amanda conceded, although

she and her pride had no intention of admitting any such thing. "I think I can survive without one."

"Uh-huh."

Deciding to quit while she was ahead, Amanda dropped the subject. Hopefully, when morning eventually rolled around everything would soon get back to normal. All she had to do was get through the night.

Not that she was thinking too much about the night to come. Not yet. One thing at a time, she told herself.

Amanda headed for the doorway to the hall. "Give me five minutes to get the children downstairs."

His low voice dogged her footsteps. "Whatever you say…sweetheart."

She resisted the urge to grind her teeth. "Thank you…dear," she said far too sweetly, leaving that statement to hang in the air as she walked out.

Chin lifted at a firm tilt, she went to round up her sisters and brothers, who she'd left gathered in Liza's room. Only Betsy greeted her with a familiar sunny expression. The rest, sitting in a row on a pale blue bedspread bordered with silver lace, wore faces pinched by worry.

"Is everything okay?" Liza asked.

"Yes," Amanda told her. "Louise is going to spend the night here because her back is a little sore, but she should be better by tomorrow." She could only hope that turned out to be the case. "I think it would be nice if we all went down and said good-night to her."

Liza helped Betsy off the bed and held her hand as they made their way to the stairs. Only Patrick hung back, dragging his feet. Amanda turned and caught his eye, which was enough to have him picking up his pace.

They found Louise still seated on the sofa with her

empty cup resting on a nearby table. "The tea was just what I needed," she told Amanda. "I'm feeling a bit more like my old self."

Her hostess wasn't sure if that was good or bad. On one hand, she wanted nothing more than Louise's swift return to excellent health. On the other, she would just as soon not be on the end of any more of the probing looks the social worker was so skilled at.

Not tonight, please.

"The children wanted to wish you a good night's rest. And," Amanda added, "I think Patrick has something special to say."

Smart boy that her brother was, he took the hint. "I'm, uh, really, really sorry."

"Then I accept your apology," Louise said in the softer tone she used wherever she spoke to the children.

"Everything's all set in the guest room," Dev informed them as he walked in. He extended a hand to Louise. "Let me help you up. We'll take it slow."

But as slow as they took it, Louise winced anyway. "Perhaps I just need to get moving again."

Dev shook his head. "Not up a flight of stairs, you don't." And with those words he carefully swung Louise into his arms in one smooth motion.

Her mouth opened, closed and opened again. "Oh, my."

His lips twitched. "Just hang on," he told the middle-aged woman who seemed stunned by the position in which she found herself. "We'll get you put to bed in no time."

With a secure grip on his burden, he started for the

hall with long, masterful strides. Louise aimed a wide-eyed look over his shoulder as they left the room.

"Oh, my," she said one more time.

IT WAS AFTER MIDNIGHT when Dev entered the house for the final time that night. Earlier, he'd made a quick trip to the drugstore for a heating pad and then had headed back to the Heartbreaker, where he'd stayed until twelve o'clock had rolled around. For once, he'd been in no hurry to come home, not when he'd more than suspected that the later he returned, the better it'd suit Amanda. It would mean they had that much less of the night to spend together.

Dev climbed the stairs to the second floor with only a small wall fixture near the top landing to light his path, feeling his frustration rise with each step. He'd been so determined to keep his mind on anything and everything but his own private needs, and in recent days he'd mostly been successful. Too bad that had come to a crashing halt this evening.

No sex. That was the deal he and Amanda had struck when he'd first proposed, and as long as she still favored that approach, he had to stick to his bargain. Trouble was, he'd never counted on being obliged to sleep—and only sleep—in the same room with her. Who the hell could have predicted that?

Well, regardless, you'll just have to cope, Devlin.

"Yeah, right. Cope," he muttered to himself as he reached the head of the stairs. He aimed a look down the hall at the newly dubbed "guest room." The door was closed and all seemed quiet in that quarter.

The door to the master bedroom was closed, as well, he noted as he headed in the opposite direction. But this time a yellow glow trickled out between the bottom of the door and the floor. Either Amanda was still awake or she'd left a light on for him.

He hoped she was asleep. He hoped she was dead to the world. Ignoring the more needy parts of him was bound to be easier if she was drifting on a cloud in dreamland, he thought, quietly opening the door.

And then he saw her.

She was asleep, all right, but not where he'd expected her to be, which was stretched out on the large pine bed big enough for a petite woman to get lost in. Instead, she was curled up in an overstuffed chair across the room, with a fluffy white blanket pulled up to her chin and her light brown hair tumbling down over her shoulders. With his gaze still locked on that sight, he shut the door behind him with a soft snap, realizing he'd never seen her hair loose before. It had always been held back by a fancy clip at the nape of her neck. All at once his fingers itched to run themselves through those long, shiny strands. In response, he fisted his hands at his sides and told himself to forget that idea—fast.

But he didn't look away.

As if she'd felt the impact of his steady stare, Amanda's eyes slowly drifted open. He could tell the second she became aware that she was no longer alone by the way her breath caught briefly before she spoke. "Did you just get home?"

"Uh-huh. Go to bed. I'll take the chair." Even those clipped words were enough to reveal a sudden huskiness he couldn't hide. Dammit.

"I'm fine here," she told him after a beat. "You're too big to sleep in the chair."

He already knew he wasn't getting a lick of sleep tonight. Every muscle in his body had gone tight. "I'm in no mood for an argument, so just take the bed, okay?"

Even as he watched, her chin went up. "Look, I don't like this situation any more than you do, but I'm trying to make the best of it. And if anyone's in the mood to argue about anything, judging by your tone, it's you."

That did it. His temper, fueled by sheer male frustration that was soaring to new heights with every breath he took, got the better of him. A few swift strides put him at the foot of the chair. With no hesitation, he reached down, picked Amanda up, blanket and all, and started across the room.

"What in the world are you—" she started to say.

Before she could finish, he dumped her in the middle of the bed. He wanted to roar out his next words. Instead, mindful of the fact that the side door to Betsy's room was open a crack, he settled for leaning in and saying them far too softly. "You're sleeping here. Live with it."

She stared up at him, her brown eyes as round as he'd ever seen them and her mouth gaping open. Finally she swallowed and regained her voice. "I think you've lost your mind," she told him, quietly yet in no uncertain terms.

He straightened and lifted a hand to rake it through his hair. "You could be right. The ways things are going, I may be an out-and-out basket case by morning."

She shoved aside the blanket, revealing the same casual top and pants she'd had on earlier. No clinging robe tonight. Dev might have been grateful—if it had made any difference, if it had made her look less desirable, if had helped ease the tension tying his gut in knots. But only one thing would help, he knew.

Slowly, inch by inch, she sat up, her gaze never

wavering from his. "I don't suppose you'd care to give me a clue as to why you're acting like this?"

There was just enough haughtiness in her tone to have his temper taking another hike. "I'll give you more than a clue," he said, beyond the point of beating around the bush. Again he leaned in, only this time he braced a knee on the side of the mattress and lowered his head until they were nose-to-nose.

"I want you," he told her in a rough whisper. "I want you now and I want you badly—so badly I ache all over."

Again she stared at him, as still as a statue, and then at last she whispered in return. "The last time…" She paused. "You agreed it was a bad idea."

"Maybe it was. Maybe it *is*. But it damn sure doesn't seem that way at the moment. It just seems…right."

As close as they were, he couldn't help but hear how her quiet breaths picked up a pace, couldn't help but see the beginnings of a soft flush forming on her cheeks, couldn't help but start to wonder if he wasn't the only one who sensed the powerful attraction ripe in the air between them. And he couldn't help but hope he wouldn't turn out to be dead wrong if he put that theory to the test. But, regardless of the consequences, he had to know.

"I want you," he said yet again. "And now the question is, do you want me?"

One second stretched to five, then ten, before she released a lengthy sigh and issued short one word that wiped out all traces of his temper even as it sent his blood racing through his veins.

"Yes."

Chapter Nine

What she had just admitted was the simple truth, Amanda recognized. A simple truth she knew could lead to a host of complications. Still, she found she had no wish to take it back, even if she could have. She hadn't been looking for it to happen, but it had happened anyway.

She wanted him, this man who'd been blunt about his own desires and, in doing so, had made her face the fact that she had some, as well—more than enough, she'd discovered in the past few minutes, to have an inner warmth spreading from tip to toe. Only a coward would deny it, and she had never been a coward.

"Yes," she repeated, more firmly this time. "I wouldn't be honest with either of us if I said otherwise."

Dev let out a lengthy breath. "You don't know how glad I am to hear that." He reached up a hand and cupped her chin. As light as his touch was, it revealed taut traces of an underlying tension, as though he were holding himself in check. "Now if you'll just say that you'll let me make love to you, maybe I won't go out of my mind, after all."

She looked into his eyes. "You want me *that* much?"

"You'd better believe it," he wasted no time in replying.

She did believe. There was no mistaking the hunger she saw in his brilliant blue gaze, and no ignoring the small, pleasurable shiver that sight sent down her spine. He wanted her. She wanted him.

But it was her choice, she knew.

She hesitated, realizing there was no going back if she did what everything female inside her urged her to do. If they became lovers, even for one night, things would change. It was only a question of how much.

Amanda ran her tongue over her lips, thinking that she might have had far less trouble resisting the chance to learn the answer if he hadn't suggested that it all seemed right to him. Even her more cautious side couldn't keep her from coming to the same conclusion. On that subject, she had to concede, she and Dev Devlin had somehow wound up in complete agreement.

And it was the *rightness* that proved to be irresistible.

"I think it would be best," she said at last, "if we made love to each other."

Those words were barely out when his mouth came down on hers. Before she could so much as blink, she found herself sprawled flat on the bed with the whole long length of him stretched out above her. The kiss was hard and deep and had them both gasping for air at its end.

"I'm not going to be able to take it slow," he muttered, his voice a rough breath of sound.

She had to smile with wry humor. "I got that impression."

He braced himself on his elbows and frowned down at her. "It'll be better next time, I promise."

Next time. So it wouldn't be just once, she thought. But then, she hadn't really expected that. "I'll try to keep up *this* time," she told him.

"Good, because I'm afraid my more demanding parts are set on breaking a few speed records." With that frank statement, he eased himself away and sat on the edge of the mattress to pull off his boots. "I'll have us both out of our clothes in less than a New York minute."

He turned out to be a man of his word, sending her top and his shirt, then her pants and his jeans, flying through air to land on the floor. "I can only be damn grateful that I moved all of my stuff here," he said.

Still wearing his dark briefs, he turned away to quickly cross the room. He crouched down to ruffle through one of the suitcases stacked against a wall. More of his belongings went flying before he found what he sought and strode back to the bed with a small bunch of foil packets in hand.

Amanda had to be grateful, as well, watching as he tossed the protection on the nightstand. She hadn't even had time to bring up the subject. No, she'd been too busy enjoying the feel of his avid hands undressing her, and now she was flat on her back again with only her white nylon bra and panties to provide a trace of modesty.

Dev stood next to the bed and stared down, letting his gaze roam over her body, his features tight. "I'm never going to last," he said, raising his eyes to meet hers.

That had her smiling again. She was discovering the undeniable thrill that came with the knowledge of being so badly desired. "You don't have to last," she replied, deciding she could be generous, "not the first time."

And then he pulled off his briefs and her breath caught in her throat. By the time her underwear went sailing across the room to join them, she was feeling far more needy than generous, so much so that she welcomed him with open arms after he applied protection and came down on top of her again. Rather than launching another kiss, he bent his head to stroke his lips over her newly revealed breasts and, despite his hurry, lingered there long enough to have her clutching his strong shoulders as her own tension grew.

"Don't wait any longer on my account," she managed to get out. Her hips moved against his with a will of their own.

"I can't wait." With that short, gritted statement, he reached down and fitted himself to her. Then he was pressing his way inside, and she had to close her eyes as tension transformed into something else entirely in the wake of his swiftly established rhythm.

Pleasure, she thought, didn't begin to describe the sensation. In fact, no word she could come up with at the moment seemed to do it justice. The only thing she knew for certain was that, whatever description would fit, she had never quite felt it before. This man, with more blunt eagerness than smoothly suave skill, was blazing a path to somewhere new, different…better.

This man. Her one-time nemesis. Her brand-new lover.

Her husband.

With his face inches above hers, Dev stared down at Amanda and clenched his teeth, calling on every scrap of control he could muster. It wasn't much.

But he had to hang on, he told himself, sensing that the woman in his arms was close to release—the same woman who'd been a thorn in his side for so long and now held the key to paradise. For all that she'd assured him he didn't have to wait for her—not the first time— he was set on doing his damnedest not go there without her. It was more than his ego at stake, he recognized. He'd always been a man who was mindful of his partner's needs as well as his own. But this time it was more than that.

He simply wanted this woman with him when he soared to the heights and made a bid to touch cloud nine. *This* woman. His former adversary. His current bedmate.

His wife.

"We'll reach the end of this road together," he told her, his husky voice now a near growl.

He knew he was risking losing it himself, but he stepped up the already rapid pace anyway, taking it to the limit in a matter of seconds. "Just let yourself go. Just—"

Suddenly her eyes flashed open and she came apart with a soft cry. In the next breath his eyes slammed shut as his own release roared through him.

Yes! he thought in triumph. *Yes!*

Then every muscle in his body went lax and his head dropped to rest alongside Amanda's. He buried his nose in her hair and let himself drift, content to bask in the rewards of sheer male satisfaction.

Eventually, reality returned. It was too soon to suit

Dev, but he knew he had to be heavy. So, with a great deal of effort, he lifted his upper body and braced his weight on his elbows. Then he gazed down at the woman stretched out under him and grinned a slow grin.

Looking delightfully rumpled and less like a practical businessperson than he'd ever seen her, she studied him for a long moment. "You seem to be in a better mood," she told him, keeping her voice low.

His grin grew. "You could say that. My insides are no longer tied up in knots…thanks to you."

"Mmm," was her only reply.

"Now you're supposed to thank me," he told her.

Again she studied him. "What makes you think thanks are in order…Mr. Macho."

For once, the nickname didn't rile him in the least. "I *know* they're in order. And I'll never call you Ms. Prim again, believe me."

That won him a small smile. "Okay. Thank you."

"You're welcome."

She released a soft sigh. "Just don't let it go to your head too much. Remember, we still have Louise to deal with in the morning, and she may not be so agreeable."

"We've got hours until morning." He lowered his head and nuzzled her cheek. "Right now, I plan to concentrate on the next time I make love to you. And then I'll be concentrating on the time after that."

Silence reigned for a second before she asked carefully, "How many times are you planning on?"

"As many as I can manage," he didn't hesitate to tell her, lifting his head. "And just so things don't get dull, I'm figuring we need to be a little…creative."

"Creative," she repeated in a slow murmur, as though testing the word.

"Uh-huh. Luckily, I remember that book you were reading a while back, the one with the, uh, interesting cover. I've got a hunch it provided more than a few inventive ideas."

She arched a brow. "Maybe I've forgotten them."

He brought his lips to hers. "Have you?" he asked against her mouth.

"No," she admitted after a beat.

He could have groaned in anticipation. Instead, he kissed her long and hard, and relished every minute of it. "You have made my night," he said at last.

She drew in a lengthy breath. "Somehow I think you could have come up with several ideas of your own."

"Do you?"

Deciding to meet the challenge, he leaned in and whispered one particular, and detailed, suggestion in her ear. He almost laughed out loud at the result it produced as she seemed to struggle to find her voice. Even when she succeeded, she only got two words out, staring straight up at him.

"Oh, my."

Now he had to chuckle, deep in his throat. "I seem to remember another female saying that earlier this evening before I carried her upstairs." He had no trouble recalling Louise's startled expression. But he wasn't thinking about her or any woman except the one he'd just made love to, he reminded himself.

Tomorrow was time enough to continue to make sure the social worker left satisfied. Tonight he was dead set on providing—and receiving—satisfaction of another sort.

AMANDA'S BRAIN was fuzzy, but her body was humming. Which was hardly surprising, she thought, after

a night filled with *creative* activities. There was no
denying that it had been an incredible experience. And
an educational one, as well, at least as far as she was
concerned. That was another thing she'd learned after
being coaxed oh-so-ardently into passing along por-
tions of the sexy novel she'd sampled.

Dev Devlin didn't need a book to give him any hints
on how to make love, inventively or otherwise.

"Good morning," Louise greeted as she entered the
kitchen. Once again dressed in her olive suit, she
looked every inch the no-nonsense government em-
ployee.

Amanda broke another egg into a glass mixing
bowl. "Good morning," she said, summoning a polite
smile. *Time to start thinking clearly,* she told herself,
and not about last night. She had to be on her toes
until Louise was safely headed back to Pine Run—and
so did the man she'd left singing a hearty tune in the
shower minutes earlier. "How are you feeling?"

"Much better," was Louise's brisk reply. "The
heating pad seems to have worked."

Amanda could have sighed in relief. "I'm so happy
to hear that," she said, and fully meant it, for more
than one reason.

"Happeee!" Betsy added from her high chair,
where she was already making inroads on her cereal.

The declaration had the social worker's mouth curving. "I suppose that makes it unanimous. As much as
I appreciate the hospitality, I'm glad that I'll be able
to be on my way soon."

It couldn't be too soon for Amanda. Still, if she
wanted to pursue the role of gracious hostess, she

knew she couldn't just shoo their visitor out the door. "You're welcome to have breakfast with us before you leave. The other children will be down in a minute. And so will my husband."

He was probably getting dressed right now, she thought. She had to concede that it was almost a shame to see him cover up that broad chest with its dusting of crisp hair, not to mention those narrow hips, muscled thighs and long legs. She'd become well acquainted with his body during the past few hours—and he with hers. She'd certainly never considered herself femme fatale material, not with a figure far more slim than curvy, but that hadn't seemed to matter. Not to the skillful lover who'd eagerly touched and tasted her. Again and again. All…night…long.

"Thank you," Louise said. "I believe I'll accept that invitation."

Amanda blinked. *What invitation?* she nearly asked before her more rational parts—not the parts that continued to hum from those nocturnal activities—reminded her that she'd offered food. She cleared her throat. "Wonderful. Please have a seat."

Moving with quick efficiency, Louise stepped over to the breakfast area and pulled out a chair next to Betsy. Another round of "good mornings" followed as the rest of the Bradley bunch filed in a second later, Rufus stalking along behind them with a powerful feline grace. Like their youngest sibling, they wore the new pajamas Amanda had helped them pick out during an earlier shopping expedition.

Contrary to her own usual morning routine, Amanda still wore her robe. On this particular day it had seemed prudent to deal with breakfast first and shower and dress later—when she'd be in no danger of being coaxed into any creative water sports by an insatiable man.

As if her thoughts had summoned him, Dev ambled in from the hall. For all that he looked comfortably laid-back in his white T-shirt and jeans, there was nothing casual about his gaze as it briefly locked on Amanda. Just as it had hours ago, a small pool of warmth spread inside her before he switched around to look at the woman seated at the table.

"How's the back?" he asked Louise. After she assured him that she was in fine shape, he grinned a wide grin as he crossed the room to retrieve a can of coffee from the refrigerator. "Nothing like a decent night's sleep to take the kinks out."

Louise studied him for a moment. "You seem awfully cheerful this morning. I suppose I'd be safe in assuming you got a good night's rest."

"Mmm." With that strictly neutral reply, he spooned dark, fragrant coffee into a gold mesh filter. "I didn't even hear my wife get out of bed this morning."

That much was true, Amanda reflected as she beat her bowl of eggs into a frothy mix. She'd gotten up and slipped out carrying a babbling Betsy while he was in the bathroom.

"She can be sneaky," he added with a sidelong glance her way. The glint in his eyes told her that if he'd been around she'd never have made it downstairs without at least a kiss. Or several of them.

Telling herself to keep her mind on the task at hand, she walked over to the stove and poured the egg mixture into a heated skillet. Before long, eggs lightly scrambled, along with cold orange juice, thick slices of hot toast and homemade strawberry jam courtesy of Mabel, were served.

For once, Amanda was also grateful for Dev's potent brand of coffee. Her first sip had her system zinging toward full alertness. Now, she thought, if she could just ignore the man seated beside her—too close beside her—maybe she could get through breakfast with her composure intact.

"The children seem to have as good an appetite this morning as they did at dinner," Louise remarked with an assessing look around the table.

"Yes," Amanda was delighted to reply. She hadn't had to worry about any of them in that respect.

"They take after their big sister," Dev said. "Of course, Amanda's appetite's not as big as mine, but it's getting there." He turned his head toward his wife. "Isn't it, sweetheart?"

His last remarks had nothing to do with food, and it was plain to her that he recognized *she* recognized it. Now she knew without a doubt why the man she'd married had once been called "Devil Devlin."

"That's right, dear," she told him calmly. She waited a deliberate beat. "But who knows, I may decide to go on a diet." She was pleased to see a fleeting frown replace his far-too-satisfied expression. It was clear he knew she wasn't talking about food, either.

Louise spoke up with typically frank directness. "Exercise is always good, but you don't need to diet."

"You can say that again," Dev agreed in no uncertain terms.

Amanda carefully lifted one shoulder in an offhand gesture and raised her coffee cup for another sip. "We'll see."

"Yeah, we certainly will," Dev muttered, and then said little else for the rest of the meal.

Louise stood up to leave shortly after they'd finished. The Devlins saw her off at the front door. "I'm sure you'll be glad to know that my report will be favorable," she told them. "And thank you again for your hospitality." With that, she left them to beat a brisk path toward her car.

"Thank goodness," Amanda said in pure relief when the door was safely closed.

"Uh-huh." Dev braced a hand on the doorjamb. His frown was back. "What did you mean by *we'll see?*"

One corner of her mouth quirked up. "Nothing much."

That's all it took for him to look every bit as relieved as she felt—for an entirely different reason, of course. "I'm guessing you've decided that you're not going to be able to keep your hands off me." He reached out and tugged her close, fitting her firmly to him. "Am I on target here?"

"Yes," she replied softly. She set aside her usual independence and laid her head on his shoulder, knowing how true it was. She wouldn't be able to deny him what he so obviously wanted. She wanted it too much herself.

No physical or emotional commitment. That had been foremost in her mind when she'd first considered a marriage in name only. And now, during the course of one night, a physical bond had been formed. Things had changed, as she'd more than suspected when she'd agreed just hours ago to make love with her husband. Her only question then had been how much.

A lot, she'd since come to believe. And now other questions were rising to take its place.

With a physical bond formed, would emotional ties follow? And what if she let that happen and found herself caring too much for a man who'd once chosen to walk on the wild side and might never truly be ready to settle down—not for a lifetime?

Logic said it could only be wise to guard against that happening. Which meant guarding her emotions...if she could.

SHE WAS HOLDING something back. Dev came to that conclusion several days after he and his wife had spent their first night together. It wasn't that Amanda denied either of them the pleasure of sharing the master bedroom—and its sprawling bed—on a regular basis. In fact, his suitcases had never made it back down the hall to what had now become a real guest room. And it wasn't that she didn't welcome him home every evening with a smile as wide as the Western sky and a kiss that could triple his pulse in a heartbeat. She did.

It was just that something seemed to be missing.

Not that he had a clue as to what it might be, he had to admit as he walked out through the Heartbreaker's swinging doors on a stormy late afternoon. It could be anything.

Or maybe it's nothing and you're all wet, Devlin.

Well, that could be true, too, he allowed. And in more ways than one.

Everything in Jester and who knew how many miles surrounding it was wet. It had been raining for forty-eight hours straight—not a drizzle, but a real downpour. Main Street, all two blocks of it, was downright waterlogged. A few customers at the saloon had joked about building an ark. Others had taken to playing mournful tunes on the jukebox. The dips and turns in the weather just had that effect on some people—maybe the majority of people when dark clouds hid even a glimmer of the sun for days on end.

But not him, Dev reflected, jamming his hands into the pockets of his long rain slicker as he started to slosh his way home. With a good dinner waiting for him and the prospect of spending another night enjoying the comforts of Amanda's silky-skinned, sweet-scented, all-female body wrapped around his, he was feeling too damn good.

It wasn't long before he found, much to his satisfaction, that his wife seemed to feel the same way. As usual these days, a generous smile curved her mouth when she caught sight of him closing the door to the entryway closet as she came down the center staircase. He crossed the living room in his stocking feet, having just dealt with his soaked boots, and met her at the bottom of the steps. There, he kissed her—and did a damn good job of it, if he did say so himself.

"I see the weather hasn't dampened any of your enthusiasm," she told him.

"Not hardly." He slid a hand down her spine and gave her soft behind a brief pat, something he'd grown fond of doing. He'd often spied other men patting their wives' backsides, but had never realized how enjoyable that simple touch could be. Until now.

Dev gave his wife another once-over, noting that she'd already changed out of what he'd come to think of as her "business clothes." Someday, he promised himself, he was going to stop in at the Ex-Libris and rumple her up good and proper when she was dressed for success. If he managed to catch her alone, he might even lock the door, herd her into the back of the store and use one of those fancy leather love seats to maximum advantage. Afterward, he could let her serve him tea in a little cup while she wore nothing but the rings he'd given her.

Oh, yeah.

Amanda studied him with an arched brow as they walked arm-in-arm down the hall toward the rear of the house. "Something tells me you're getting hungry."

He swallowed a chuckle. "I am." *In more ways than one.* "What's for dinner?"

"Beef stew. I thought something hearty was in order with all the gloom and doom outside. I have to admit that I hope the sun puts in an appearance soon. This constant rain seems to be getting the children down."

Dev discovered how true that was after Amanda headed off to the kitchen and he stepped into the family room. As usual for this time of day, the kids were stretched out on the rug, watching TV before dinner. The laugh track of an old sitcom provided a cheery background to what was happening on the screen, but none of its viewers looked all that happy.

"Hi, guys," he said in a deliberately upbeat voice.

He got three quiet greetings in return as he settled himself on the sofa. Betsy merely stood and teetered over to him. He waited for a familiar demand to pick her up, but she just laid her curly blond head on his denim-clad knees. Reaching down, he gently placed her in his lap. He was so used to seeing a sunny grin that he immediately noticed its lack as she sighed and settled back against his chest. For a second he wondered if she might be sick and felt helpless at the thought. He had zip experience in dealing with a sick child.

But Amanda was a lot more likely to know if anything was seriously wrong, he assured himself in the next breath. If she wasn't worried, he shouldn't be, either.

Right from the first, she'd taken to the role of mother to her sisters and brothers, and she was still doing a bang-up job. He, on the other hand, was still mostly a bystander when it came to taking care of the kids on a day-to-day basis. Which, of course, was the way she'd planned it. She didn't expect him to take care of the kids. She didn't expect him to be involved much at all with them beyond the fact that he was their big sister's husband. She probably didn't even expect him to try to cheer them up.

Trouble was, he flat-out hated to see them so glum.

"I know you probably all miss going out in the backyard and running around," he told them, "but it can't rain forever."

Caleb turned away from the television. "I think it's been forever already."

"Hmm." Deciding to take another tack, Dev asked, "How was kindergarten today?"

Caleb gave his head a disgusted shake. "One girl kept hangin' on to me every time it thundered—" he made a face "—and we all had to stay inside at recess."

"That's too bad," Dev agreed. He didn't think it was the time to tell Caleb that someday girls hanging on to him would be good.

"Me and Betsy hadda stay inside all day," Patrick muttered, deserting the sitcom to air his own grievances. "We can't even go to school."

"But I'll bet Mabel baked something," Dev countered.

"Yeah. She called it a pound cake. It was pretty good."

Obviously not good enough, though, Dev thought, to make up for another round of dark skies. "How about you, Liza? How was your day?"

The oldest Bradley child picked up the remote and flicked off the television. "It was all right," she said in her typically quiet fashion.

Dev ran his tongue over his teeth. "Just all right, huh?" At Liza's small shrug, he added, "Well, I'm beginning to suspect that Betsy's not her usual happy self because the rest of you are on the glum side. Maybe it's time to start feeling better."

"I guess so," Liza allowed after a second. She gave her brothers a sober look. "We don't want to make Betsy sad."

Caleb offered a solemn nod. "Okay."

Patrick ducked his head. "Yeah."

"So smile," Dev told them in a hearty tone.

They did. And none of the three looked all that much cheerier. Betsy merely issued another sigh, evidently agreeing.

By the time everyone sat down to dinner, Dev had almost given up on changing the situation. Maybe he should just join Amanda in hoping that the skies would clear soon, he told himself. After all, he'd had his glum moments as a kid and he'd gotten over them.

For a while, as he recalled, his big grievance had been rules. There'd always seemed to be so many rules made up by people a lot bigger than you were. Once upon a time, his dream had been a world with no rul—

Dev stopped with his fork poised halfway to his mouth as an idea hit. After a second's consideration, he decided it was worth a shot. With any luck at all, it just might produce some badly lacking cheer.

He looked across the table at Amanda. "I've got a notion on how to perk the kids up." *Just go along with me,* he did his best to convey with a meaningful lift of a brow.

Amanda pursed her lips. She'd gotten the gist of his silent message. He was seeking her cooperation in whatever notion he'd come up with.

"What I'm suggesting," he added, aiming a glance around the table, "is a no-rules evening."

Everyone except the littlest Bradley, who was busy making mincemeat out of her dinner roll, stared back at him. Finally, Amanda spoke. "A *no-rules* evening?" she repeated carefully.

"Uh-huh." Dev set his fork down. "For one evening, everybody's allowed to break some rules." He switched his gaze to Caleb. "For instance, if Caleb wants to push all the carrots aside before he eats the rest of his stew, he can—just for tonight."

"I *can?*" The boy's brown eyes went as round as one of Mabel's chocolate cookies.

"If your big sister agrees with the plan," Dev told him.

Caleb looked at Amanda. "Do you, Mandy?"

His young face held so much hope. Amanda didn't even ask herself if she could turn him down and watch it fade. She knew she couldn't. Not this time.

"Just for tonight," she said, "I suppose we can all break a few rules." Seeing the blinding smile her agreement produced, she simply couldn't regret it.

"Holy cow!" Still smiling to beat the band, Caleb wasted no time in starting to shove his carrots to the far side of his plate.

After that, things moved along quickly. Liza, with only a little coaxing, asked to be allowed to give Rufus his own plate of stew, and the cat, who seemed to have a sixth sense for timing his appearances to coincide with food on the table, relished every bite. Dev, with a devilish look his wife's way, chose not to deal with the dirty dishes once dinner was over, and Amanda, getting into the spirit of the thing, absolved herself of any responsibility for serving dessert, leaving that task to her husband. Then Patrick elected not to take a bath—or wash behind his ears—and both boys had forbidden slides down the banister supervised by Amanda at the top of the long pine staircase and Dev at the bottom.

At last it was Betsy's turn, but no one could come up with anything against the rules that she'd been pining to do. "Well, she likes to go up," Dev said at length. "Let's put her way up." And with that, he settled the little girl on his shoulders, which turned out to be much to her delight. Now she wasn't only cheerfully babbling, her good humor long since restored, but giggling nonstop as he made a tour of the home's lower level with the rest of the group following behind.

"It's getting late," Amanda said when they finally climbed the steps to the second floor. "I think this concludes our no-rules evening."

Dev halted at the top of the stairs with Betsy still perched high. "Maybe not quite." His gaze settled on Liza. "When you made your choice earlier, you did it for Rufus, and I hope that cat knows how lucky he is to get a whole plate of stew for himself. But don't you have something you'd like to do for *you?*"

Amanda laid a gentle hand on the girl's narrow

shoulder and gave it a reassuring squeeze. "That's right. You still get to choose, if you want to."

Liza peeked up at her. A few quiet seconds passed before she spoke. "Could I...jump on the bed—just once?"

"That's a *super* idea," Caleb said. "Can we all jump on the bed?"

Amanda released a soft sigh. "I suppose you can."

"Whoopee!" Patrick cried.

"I guess," Dev slid in, his tone wry, "we'll have to find a big bed."

"Mmm-hmm." Amanda turned and started for the master bedroom. "I'll lead the way this time."

Before long all four children were jumping up and down on the large bed in their stocking-clad feet. The boys hooted and hollered. Betsy giggled up a storm.

And Liza, bouncing even higher than the rest of her siblings, gradually smiled, then eventually grinned, and then finally laughed out loud.

It was music to Amanda's ears. Thank goodness, she thought as the last of her lingering worries about the eldest of the Bradley bunch faded. Liza might always be on the serious side, but she could let herself go and laugh, too. She hadn't lost the ability to enjoy just being a child.

Things were going to be all right. Thank goodness.

Amanda turned toward the man who stood beside her, prepared to share her conclusions, but the expression on his face had her voice dying in her throat. Although she couldn't make out what he might be thinking, he looked so caught up in watching the children. It wasn't long before she found herself caught up in watching him.

He was the one who'd worked wonders tonight, she

thought. Leave it to a former bad boy to come up with an evening dedicated to breaking rules. Not that he bore much resemblance to a bad boy at the moment, she had to concede. Instead, he looked like a full-grown male who was… *Captivated* might be the word. Not by the action in progress, surely. She more than suspected that the young Dev Devlin had been no stranger to the forbidden joys of bed-jumping.

But if it wasn't what the children were doing that had such a lock on his attention, the only alternative seemed to be the children themselves. One thing for certain, she had never seen that look on his face before. She'd seen him angry at times, amused at others and, just lately, thoroughly aroused in a way that could steal her breath. But the expression he wore now was brand-new.

Amanda couldn't help but wonder what it meant.

Chapter Ten

He'd tumbled for them like a ton of stacked hay bowled over by a strong wind. One minute he'd simply been enjoying the sight of the kids having a rip-roaring good time bouncing on that bed, and the next something gut deep in him had seemed to shift gears. The upshot was that he'd found himself no longer only determined to keep those four towheads safe. Sure, he'd still do his best to protect them, no matter what. But by the end of their no-rules evening more than protective instincts had kicked in.

Unless he missed his guess, the Bradley kids had got through what he'd always figured was some pretty thick skin and burrowed straight inside him. *Maybe,* something told him, *they made it far enough to wiggle their way into your heart.*

Whatever the case, for the first time he'd begun to think that stepping into a parent's shoes might not be beyond him, despite the fact that his own parents had never provided even a passable example of how to go about it. Maybe he *could* get a handle on it. The kids seemed to like him well enough, so they just might give him the chance.

But would Amanda?

That question rumbled through Dev's mind as he lounged back on an old wooden bench in Jester Community Park on a Saturday morning that had thankfully dawned at least clear enough to hold little threat of more rain. It had occurred to him more and more over the course of the past few days that he was far from sure how Amanda felt about him, even though they'd become as physically close as two people could probably get. She still wanted him, that was plain enough, but anything beyond that was by and large a mystery.

Then again, how do you feel about her, Devlin?

Another hell of a question, he had to admit. He still had trouble keeping his hands off her, that was for sure, and he had more than a hunch that wouldn't change anytime soon. When it came to other things, though, he was a lot less certain of the answer. The truth was, like many males of his acquaintance, he'd never been at his best when it came to figuring out relationships with the female half of the population. For all that he'd been a husband for weeks now, he was still groping his way.

But he was hopeful he'd get better at it. He had to be optimistic, he told himself. Could be that before too long he and Amanda would start discussing the future, and, who knew, she just might give him the chance to be a real parent to her sisters and brothers. Could be, in fact, that they'd all wind up living happily ever after.

Dev had to grin as that last thought hit. "Talk about optimism," he murmured under his breath. "If you're not careful, Devlin, you'll wind up with stars in your eyes."

Then again, what could it hurt to look on the bright

side? he asked himself with a light shrug. The rain seemed to be over for a while. The kids were back to normal. And best of all, he reflected as his grin widened, he was already having a good time spending a few hours alone with the two Bradley boys. Their big sister had clearly been startled when he'd asked them over breakfast if they wanted to join him for some baseball practice at the park, but the boys had wasted no time in accepting the invitation, so she'd only nodded her agreement.

A little male bonding, he thought, was a start.

"Did something used to be there?" Caleb asked from his seat beside Dev. He pointed to a large slab of bare concrete near the pond.

"Uh-huh. That was where the pavilion stood."

"The what?"

"The pavilion," Dev repeated. "It's a kind of building that has no walls, just a big roof. It fell down a while ago."

Not accidentally, either, he added to himself, recalling the sheriff's announcement that had created a buzz all over town. In the aftermath of those findings, had Luke McNeil come to the same conclusion he himself had about the fire that had started in the wreckage after the collapse? Dev wondered. Probably. It was pretty plain in hindsight that whoever had sabotaged the pavilion had resorted to arson to try to hide the evidence. Luckily Jester's volunteer Fire and Rescue squad, of which Dev was a member, had quickly put out the blaze without much harm done. Now, with the wreckage hauled away, the building that had been a big part of the town's Founders' Day celebration every March was history—and the guilty party was still on the loose.

"Break time's about over," Dev told his companions, reaching up to tap down his Stetson. "Ready to take a few more swings?"

"Sure." Caleb finished the last of his candy bar and hopped to his feet. He picked up the small bat Dev had bought at the Mercantile that morning along with three chocolate bars to tide them over until lunch and new hats for the boys.

"All right, I'll pitch," Dev said, rising. He tossed the ball he'd been holding in the air and caught it with a snap of his wrist. "You take the outfield, Patrick."

"Okay." Patrick tugged down the brim of the straw cowboy hat that had struck his fancy. Unlike his older brother, the four-year-old had turned down the chance to pick out a baseball cap. His miniature ranch hadn't only become his favorite toy, it seemed he favored all things Western. It probably wouldn't be long before the kid would want some boots, too.

And Dev promised himself he'd see Patrick got them, even if Amanda rolled her eyes at his buying more stuff. He liked giving things to all the kids.

They jogged back to the small practice diamond at one side of the larger ball field. Caleb took his place at home plate. They had this part of the park to themselves at the moment. A few birds chattered in nearby trees and some soft voices could be heard coming from a children's play area closer to where the park ended at Lottery Lane, but for the most part it was quiet.

"Ready?" Dev asked Caleb.

"Yep."

Dev launched the ball in an underhand toss, making sure he didn't get too much speed on it. Caleb swung and the bat connected with a soft crack.

"Holy cow!" Caleb said as Dev whipped around to

see the ball fly farther than anything else the boy had hit so far. "I'm gettin' good."

Dev watched Patrick take off after it. He judged that with the way the ball had landed and started to roll at a fast clip it would be a while before the kid returned. "Why don't you give your brother a hand tracking it down," he told Caleb. "You guys can play catch on the way back."

Caleb didn't hesitate to follow up on that suggestion, using his running shoes to maximum advantage.

Another grin curved Dev's mouth. They were getting some exercise for sure, he thought. Even with his limited childcare experience, he knew that had to be good. Maybe that was why he felt so good himself, just watching them.

"See you're out getting some fresh air," a deep voice said in a hearty tone.

Dev didn't even have to look to know who that robust voice belonged to. Jester's duly elected mayor usually spoke as if he were making a speech at Town Hall.

"Morning, Bobby," Dev said mildly. He switched his gaze to the big, brown-haired man just in time to catch the fleeting frown that greeting produced. Ever since the lottery win had brought a load of publicity down on the town's head, Bobby Larson had taken to calling himself "Robert." But Dev wasn't about to chime in. In fact, he'd only go so far as to allow that *big* was the word to describe most everything about the mayor.

Bobby, a good-old-boy type in his late forties, favored sport coats with checks so big he looked like a walking checkerboard half the time. He drove a big gold Cadillac that had once been top-of-the-line but had long since faded to a shadow of its former glory. And he had big schemes for how to put Jester on the map in a major way.

Predictably, in the manner of a born politician, Bobby hid his irritation and smiled a wide smile, teeth gleaming like the silver streaks at his temples. "Haven't heard much from you about my plans to really make something of this place." He took in the area where they stood with a sweeping gesture.

Dev glanced around the park. Maybe because of the Bradley boys he could see enjoying a game of catch in the distance, his thoughts went back to his own days as a child. Even when things had been a lot less than happy at home, he recalled how he'd been able to enjoy himself here. More than just a place to play, it had been a haven, he recognized for the first time.

"Once we get a high-class hotel built on this land," Bobby said, "the tourists will start flocking in. The economy's going to shoot right through the roof."

"And what about the kids?" Dev asked quietly.

Bobby looked at him. "The kids?"

"Where will they play if the park is gone?"

The mayor shrugged a broad shoulder. "They'll find somewhere else, most likely. I'm sure you wouldn't be in favor of stopping progress. You're a businessman, after all."

Dev could hardly argue that last point. He was a businessman, all right. He was also someone who'd been bound and determined to steer clear of local politics, he reminded himself. That's why he'd avoided taking sides when it came to furthering or opposing Bobby Larson's schemes. Instead, he'd vowed to concentrate on the Heartbreaker and maintain a neutral stance.

But now, Dev knew, he was going to break that vow.

"Progress isn't everything," he said firmly. "Folks in town need this park, and that makes it more important."

For a moment Bobby looked startled. His smile faltered before he pasted it back on his face. "Come on, you don't really mean that."

"The hell I don't," was Dev's blunt reply.

Bobby's smile deserted him in a flash. "In that case, I'll leave you to your fresh air and be on my way. I've got *business* to attend to." Whipping around, he headed back past the basketball courts bordering the baseball field. "Might've known I couldn't expect much," he muttered just loud enough to be heard, "not from one of the no-account Devlins."

Dev fisted his hands at his sides and counted to ten. It was either that or stalk after Jester's mayor and kick him flat in his beefy butt. *The no-account Devlins.* It had been a long time since he'd actually heard those once-familiar words spoken by one of Jester's citizens, so long that he'd almost believed he might never hear them again.

Fat chance.

"It's my turn to be batter," Patrick said as the boys came running up.

"That's right." Dev's good mood had gone downhill in a hurry, but he told himself he wouldn't let that spoil the kids' fun. For the next hour he kept a smile on his face. Even though to another adult it might have looked as forced around the edges as Bobby's last effort, the boys didn't seem to notice.

When the sun peeking through the scattered clouds was near its high point in the sky, they left the park and headed for the Brimming Cup. Rather than fixing a midday meal as usual when Amanda was working, Mabel had agreed to take the Bradley girls for a visit to the bookstore, after which everyone would meet at the diner for lunch.

Dev and the boys passed the Medical Center and Jester Public Library as they made their way down Lottery Lane. Olivia Mason, a slender woman in her early forties, waved a greeting from across the street before continuing on her way.

"She's a teacher at my school," Caleb told his brother.

"Next year I get to go," Patrick announced with a proud set of his narrow shoulders.

Caleb looked at Dev. "Did you go to my school, too?"

"Uh-huh." *And I was a trial to more than one of my teachers,* Dev acknowledged to himself, although he didn't pass that news along. "Might as well make a quick detour to the post office and see if we've got any mail," he said instead.

They waited for Jester's only stoplight to turn green and crossed Main Street, then passed the grocery store and the hair salon. The post office was located in a small building next to the sheriff's office, and it rivaled the local barbershop as the hub of town gossip. With that in mind, Dev wasn't surprised to see Wyla Thorpe standing at the counter talking a mile a minute to Bernice Simms, the town's veteran postmistress. The string-bean-thin redhead with a knack for making a pest of herself and the stout gray-haired woman responsible for the local mails were a stark contrast, even down to their speech patterns. One whined, the other bubbled.

Dev ignored the whining Wyla and concentrated on Bernice, who offered a lively greeting. It hardly amazed him when the boys followed his example, or when Wyla, clearly miffed at the inattention, sailed out with an irritated sniff.

"I have something for you," Bernice told Dev. She reached into one of the wooden slots behind her and pulled out a letter. "Not much today, but at least it doesn't seem to be a bill," she said, handing it over.

Dev glanced down at the letter while Bernice chatted with the boys. It had a Nevada postmark and no return address, but he didn't need one to more than suspect who'd sent it. His older brother's scrawling handwriting hadn't changed much, even after all the years Jed Jr. had been away who knew where.

Dev tore the envelope open and pulled out a single sheet of white paper. He only had to read a few sentences to have his mood, already none too good after his encounter with the mayor, taking a sharp dive for the worse.

"I hope it's not bad news," Bernice said after he'd finished the letter and replaced it in the envelope.

"It could be better," Dev allowed in the most offhand tone he could muster. "Let's go, guys," he added to the boys, shoving the envelope into a back pocket of his jeans.

Jeez, he thought as they headed out and found a stray dark cloud passing overhead to cast gloom over the old Main Street storefronts. *Jeez, Jed Jr., how could you screw up this badly?*

SOMETHING WAS WRONG. Amanda knew it after one look at the set-in-stone expression on her husband's face as he walked into the Brimming Cup with Caleb and Patrick leading the way. She couldn't deny that he'd caught her off guard when he'd offered to take the boys to the park that morning. Now, despite the fact that her brothers seemed far from upset themselves as they hurried forward after catching sight of her seated in one of the diner's large fifties-style booths, she had to wonder whether she'd been wise to let them accept that invitation.

"Hi!" The boys said in unison.

Amanda slid off a length of light blue vinyl and stood up. On the other side of the booth, Mabel remained seated with Liza beside her. "You can sit here," Amanda told the boys, indicating the space she'd left open.

She took a small bat from Caleb and a ball from Patrick. "I'll put these up in front until we leave." As they scrambled in, she turned to Dev. "Did everything go all right at the park?" she asked, dropping her voice.

He gazed down at her, his eyes shaded by the rim of his Stetson. "Everything went fine. I think they had a great time."

She glanced back at her brothers. They were chatting up a storm with Liza and Mabel while Betsy viewed the conversation from a high chair standing near the end of the booth. "You didn't have to buy them new hats."

"I know. I wanted to." His even tone revealed no more than his gaze.

She cleared her throat. "Well, why don't you scoot in next to the boys and I'll sit by Mabel."

He shook his head. "I'm not real hungry at the moment and I should get over to the Heartbreaker. Roy's about to open up."

She considered reminding him that they'd agreed to all have lunch together, then thought better of it. "Okay, I'll explain to Mabel and the children that you had to leave."

"Thanks," he said. And that was all he said before he turned and wasted little time in walking out.

Amanda swallowed a sigh and explained Dev's departure as best she could. Her sisters and brothers accepted it at face value. Mabel, on the other hand, looked curious, although she merely aimed a glance around the booth and asked, "Well, what are you children going to have?"

Leaving them to discuss the merits of hamburgers versus macaroni and cheese, Amanda took the bat and ball to the front counter, where Shelly was ringing up a customer with a typically warm smile. Once the diner's owner was free, Amanda stepped forward. "Can you put these behind the counter until we're through with lunch?"

"Sure." Shelly took the bat and ball and placed them under the long, gray Formica counter. "Now I've got a question for you," she said, looking straight at Amanda. "What's the matter with Dev? He didn't even say hello to me when he walked in—or goodbye when he left. That certainly isn't like him."

And trust Shelly to notice, Amanda thought, studying her friend. As usual, she found it hard not to be candid with the woman who wore a yellow blouse under her apron today but would probably be switching to maternity tops in the near future. They'd simply known each other too well for too long.

"I'm only sure that something *is* the matter," she said, keeping her voice low.

"Hmm." Shelly arched a brown brow. "Marital problems?"

Amanda gave her head a quick shake. "We've actually been getting along fine."

"*Fine?* Well, that's a change. Still," Shelly added after a moment, "maintaining a marriage in name only would probably be harder for a man than a woman. Sometimes those big, strapping males are more, ah, needy in certain areas than we are."

"That's not the problem," Amanda replied, getting her friend's drift.

"Sure?"

"Positive."

Shelly's hazel eyes took on a knowing glint. "I'd say there's only one way you could be positive…and that would be if it's no longer a marriage in name only."

Amanda blew out a breath, unable to refute that logic. "Okay, so it's not."

Shelly grinned, obviously as pleased as punch at the news. "I told you he was too darn good-looking to live with and resist for any length of time."

"Well, you were right," Amanda admitted.

"Since you're being so generous in conceding my wisdom," Shelly said, "I suppose I'll have to forgive you for running off to get hitched at the courthouse, even though I would have loved to see you get married."

"It wasn't," Amanda told her, "that big of a deal." Nothing like her friend's wedding a few months ago, with many of the town's residents in attendance.

"Weddings," Shelly firmly contended, "should be a big deal."

"Is anybody gonna pick up this meatloaf platter in

the next year or two?'' the diner's cook called out at that point, his gruff voice coming from the pass-through to the kitchen. Dan Bertram, who'd been at the Brimming Cup long enough to become as much of a fixture as the row of chrome-legged stools favored by some of its regulars, knew his way around a sizzling grill, but patience wasn't always his strong suit.

"Keep your shirt on, Dan," Shelly called back, "I'm coming." Dropping her voice, she continued. "Dev may be out of sorts about something, Amanda, but that probably won't last. I don't think there's anything to worry about. In fact, everything may be back to normal by dinnertime."

UNFORTUNATELY Shelly's prediction proved to be anything but accurate. Dinnertime had come and gone, Amanda thought later that evening as she dressed for bed, and things were still far from normal. Her husband had been quiet at dinner, leaving her and the children to keep the conversation going, and then he'd headed back to the Heartbreaker as soon as their meal was over. She had no idea how late it would be before he returned for the night, but she'd promised herself she would stay up for as long as it took in order to talk to him alone.

Something was wrong, and she was determined to learn as much as she could, no matter what.

Amanda tightened the belt on her long satin robe and decided to make herself comfortable in one of the twin bedroom chairs—the same chair Dev hadn't let her sleep in the first night they'd shared this room. The first night they'd made love. The first night she'd fully discovered her own capacity for giving and receiving pleasure. Her pulse fluttered in her veins just thinking about it.

But she wouldn't be carried off to bed for a repeat performance, she vowed. Not tonight. Not until she'd found out a few things.

She wasn't sure how much time passed before the bedroom door opened and Dev walked in. "I thought you might be in bed," he said quietly, shutting the door behind him. He wore the same closed expression that had become so familiar that day.

Amanda folded her arms under her breasts, deciding there was no point in beating around the bush. "Neither of us is going to bed until you tell me what's bothering you." It was as firm a statement as she could make it.

He studied her for a long moment, as though gauging the strength of her will. "Why do I have the feeling you're not backing down on that come hell or high water?" he asked at last.

"Because it's the truth."

After another moment of sheer silence, he heaved a gusty sigh, crossed the room, and settled himself in the overstuffed chair beside hers. "It would be simpler if we just went to bed. Sure I can't convince you?"

Sitting forward, she ignored that question in favor of her own. "What's wrong?"

He leaned back and stacked a booted foot on a denim-clad knee. "Well, for starters," he said, "I had a run-in with our mayor while I was at the park this morning. He started touting the virtues of his idea to build a hotel on park land, and I basically told him I thought his plan stunk."

That news came as a surprise to Amanda. Several people in town had been vocal about their opposition to the hotel, but not the Heartbreaker Saloon's owner. "As far as I know, you've never voiced that opinion before."

"It was a first," he agreed. "Bobby didn't take kindly to it, either."

"No, I can imagine he wouldn't." She paused, sure there had to be more to the story to produce the reaction it had. *For starters*. That's what he'd said a minute ago, she reminded herself. "And then what happened?"

His jaw tightened. "Bobby took off in a snit, but not before getting in a pointed dig about the good-for-nothing Devlins." He crossed his arms over the row of silver snaps down the front of his stonewashed-blue shirt. "Cripes, I grew up hearing variations on the same theme. Not that I helped matters any back then, I'll admit, by sticking my chin out every time it happened and just looking for ways to get into more trouble."

"Yes, and from all of the stories I've heard, you generally found it," she allowed, deciding to go with the simple truth. "But that all changed years ago."

Although he chuckled low in his throat, the sound held little humor. "That's what I told myself when I bought the Heartbreaker, that I was turning my life around. After today, though, I'm more of the opinion that I'll never really escape."

His last words captured her attention. "Escape?" she repeated quietly.

"What I came from."

What I came from. Amanda frowned as that stark statement echoed in her mind. "If you mean your family background," she said after a moment, "regardless of whatever comment the mayor made, none of that applies to you now. It's all in the past."

Dev gave his head a slow shake. "Trouble is, it's not all in the past. I found that out today." He hesitated for the barest instant, then continued. "The kids and I stopped at the post office on our way to the diner. There was a letter from my brother waiting for me."

Her frown deepened. Whatever that letter had contained, she reflected, it had to be far from good news. In fact, she was all but positive that this was what had put that set-in-stone expression on her husband's face earlier.

"How is your brother?" she asked, keeping her tone mild.

His unflinching gaze met hers. "Not great. He's in jail in Nevada after being convicted on several counts of burglary last year. A sneak thief, that's how Jed Jr. wound up. Just," he added with a rueful twist of his lips, "what more than a few folks in this town would once have expected of a no-account Devlin."

Amanda took in what he'd told her and sought a response. "You're not your brother," she said at last. "Or anyone else in your family, for that matter. You're you."

"Humph." He raised a hand and ran it through his hair. "That sounds so reasonable when you say it, but you're not coming from the same place I am, believe me. You're a Bradley, after all. The good citizens of Jester—at least some of them—must have figured you married beneath you when you picked me for a husband."

There'd been a time when she wouldn't have so much as considered the possibility of defending someone she'd regarded as her cross to bear. Now her spine straightened in the blink of an eye. "If anyone is ever so foolish as to say anything along those lines to me," she huffed out, "I'll set them straight in a hurry."

That had his mouth slanting up at the tips. "Thanks. I appreciate it." Then even that faint smile she'd won from him disappeared. "Nonetheless, we both know the Bradleys and the Devlins are an unlikely mix, to say the least."

Again Amanda found herself groping for a response. "My own family had its less-than-sterling moments," she reminded him. It had taken months, she recalled, for gossip to die down after Sherman Bradley had run off with Rita Winslow.

As if he knew full well what she was thinking, Dev said, "I suppose everyone's allowed one case of bad judgment, no matter how many tongues it sets wagging. My relatives, on the other hand, seem to have made a career of getting themselves talked about. And now we've got a jailbird in the Devlin clan—a first even for us, I have to concede."

With that, he surged to his feet and began to pace, as though unable to sit still any longer. The soft glow of the small lamp Amanda had switched on earlier emphasized the hard lines of his face. "Hell, if there is such a thing as bad blood," he said, "I guess I've got my share."

Amanda heard the disgust clear in his voice. But it was the thin edge of despair underscoring it that tugged at something deep at the core of her.

His earlier comment about his fading hopes for escape had been no idle one, she realized. He truly was beginning to believe he'd never be able to live down a family history familiar to many of Jester's residents. For the first time she recognized how important that had become to him. Despite the fact that his last name was Devlin, he wanted the town's respect. The same basic respect she herself had always enjoyed…as a Bradley.

He had no way of knowing that the Bradleys and Devlins had more in common than he could ever have imagined. Of all of Jester's citizens, only she knew that.

So do you tell him?

Amanda released a long breath, wondering if she could do it, if she could share what she'd been determined to keep private ever since the phone call from the lawyer in Pine Run telling her about her sisters and brothers while also offering some tragic news about her—their—father.

And, as informative as that conversation had been, it wasn't even the whole of it, she acknowledged. For years—ten years to be exact—she'd kept to herself some candid facts her dying mother had passed along to her. Again they related to her father, and again Sherman Bradley's daughter had deemed them too personal to reveal.

It wouldn't be easy to break her silence now, she knew. But then, could she take the easy way out and leave the man who continued to pace in front of her clueless when revealing a few unwelcome truths might help him?

No, she decided, taking the easy way out simply wouldn't work. Not tonight.

"I know it must have been a quite a jolt to find out about your brother," she said at last, "but you're not the only one in this room who has a convicted criminal in the family."

He halted in midstep and looked down at her with a puzzled frown. "What do you mean?"

Her gaze locked with his. "I mean," she told him, "that my father died in prison."

Chapter Eleven

Dev went stock-still as every muscle in his body tensed for a humming instant. Maybe he hadn't heard right, was his first thought. But, hard on the heels of that reflection, the stark look clear as glass in Amanda's eyes told him he had.

"Your dad went to jail," he said, making it a statement rather than question.

"Yes." Her gaze didn't waver. "He was convicted of embezzling money from a bank he worked for in Minnesota. I found out about it at the same time I learned of the children he'd fathered after he left Montana."

Hunkering down in one slow motion, he cupped his palms around knees covered by the clinging folds of the dusky rose robe he liked to see his wife wearing—almost he much as he liked taking it off her. But he wasn't thinking about that now.

"It must have been a shock," he said as gently as he could manage.

"In some ways it was," she replied, setting her far smaller hands on top of his. "And it some ways it wasn't."

He couldn't figure that one out. "Why weren't you shocked straight through?"

"Because my father had a gambling addiction. In fact, he'd had it for years before he even went to Minnesota."

Dev felt his brows hike up of their own accord. "Well, I'll be damned. I never so much as suspected that," he admitted with blunt directness.

"Neither did I," she acknowledged with equal frankness. "I didn't know it until I came home from college to be with my mother during her last illness. I'd wondered why Mom didn't seem quite as amazed as everyone else when my father ran off. A part of me almost resented the fact that she took it as calmly as she did. He was barely gone when she started making plans to work out of our home as a seamstress to supplement what money my father left her."

Amanda drew in a quiet breath. "Then, shortly before she died, she took me into her confidence, and I discovered that she hadn't had it easy being married to a man who not only secretly craved risks, but who it was risky to rely on—something my mother recognized even before my father ran off without a word."

"Well, I'll be dam—" Dev started to say one more time.

"There's more," Amanda told him, breaking in. "You may as well know that my father didn't buy the space next to the Heartbreaker from your uncle for investment purposes as most people, including me, believed at the time. According to my mother, he won it in a private poker game that took place one night after the saloon was closed with your uncle and some of his friends, all of whom have long since left town."

Well, in a way that made sense, Dev thought, recalling how his uncle had always shied away from discussing that "sale." Back then, he'd assumed his father's younger brother had simply needed a quick influx of cash. Now he knew the saloon's former owner, who'd prided himself at being handy with a deck of cards, was reluctant to reveal to his nephew— or anyone else—that he'd been bested by Amanda's father.

"You didn't have to tell me all this," he said, more than suspecting how difficult it must been for her.

"No," she acknowledged, still looking straight into his eyes, "but I couldn't let you go on thinking that you're the only one in town with a thief for a relative. The fact that my father's crime was a white-collar version he finally resorted to because he couldn't kick his gambling habit makes little difference. In the end, your brother and my father both stole something that didn't belong to them."

She pulled her hands from his and set them back in her lap. "And who knows, maybe your brother will see things in a different light by the time he's released and not end up as my father did, withering away in a matter of months because he simply couldn't stand being behind bars and thinking about what he'd done to himself and the new family he formed after leaving Jester."

Dev straightened to his full height and took a short step back. "Thanks for telling me."

She rose from the chair. "Did it help?"

"Yeah, it did," he replied as he slid his arms around her waist and pulled her to him, recognizing it was the sheer truth. He felt better—a lot better—than he had in several long and dismal hours.

And he owed it all to his wife.

Maybe that was why he felt not only better but closer to her, as well. Not just physically, but... Hell, he couldn't describe it. He wanted her, that much he knew full well. Now, though, something was telling him that somewhere along the way he'd started needing her, too.

He'd wanted other women in the past. He'd be lying through his teeth if he said otherwise. Needing a woman, however, was a whole different story, especially when only one particular female seemed to be able to fill the bill.

"Can we go to bed now?" he asked as the familiar wanting and the brand-new need joined forces to jump-start his pulse.

A wry smile tugged at the corners of her mouth. "Are you sleepy?"

"Not hardly." His voice had gone from low to downright husky in a split second.

Something that might have been amusement began to dance in her eyes. "I could fix you a cup of warm milk."

"I'm already warm," he told her. He switched their positions in one swift turn and started walking her backward toward his goal. "In fact, my temperature's on the rise."

"Could be a fever."

He kept them moving. "Oh, it's a fever, all right. And I'm counting on you to do something about it."

"Hmm." She came up against the bed. "Maybe we should get you out of your clothes first."

"Good thinking."

Her fingers went to work on the snaps of his shirt. It wasn't long before she had it off him. "Your boots should probably come next. Why don't you sit on the bed and I'll deal with them?''

He wasn't about to argue. He was too busy being aroused by the fact that she seemed far from reluctant to strip him down to bare skin. He'd usually been the one to take the lead and undress them both. This, he decided, made a damn fine change of pace.

''Time to stretch out on the bed,'' Amanda told him moments later as she finished her task by sending his dark briefs dropping to the floor.

He flipped the bedspread back and did as instructed, then watched as she removed her robe and nightgown. He tried not to let himself get too churned up at the sight of all the creamy skin being gradually revealed. He wanted to take this slow and easy and make it last.

Then she eased herself down on top of him and he wondered if slow was that important, after all. ''You feel so soft and smooth,'' he told her, clutching her gently curved hips to hold her fast to him.

She propped her elbows on his chest. ''You feel rock solid—'' she wiggled a little ''—all over.''

He sucked in a ragged breath. ''If I take charge, this is going to be over in one minute flat. How about if I just lay back and let you ravish me?''

''Ravish you?'' She mulled that idea over and began to look intrigued. ''I suppose it could have its merits.''

''Definitely,'' he assured her.

She hesitated for a scant second, then nodded. ''All right, I'll do my best.''

And she did.

First with her small hands, then with her soft lips, she brought him to the brink of losing his control, until he was grasping the sheets with hard fists in a bid to hang on, just hang on for a little while longer. The most male parts of him didn't help matters by silently urging him to bring things to a satisfying conclusion—*now*. Finally, he groped to retrieve a foil packet from the nightstand drawer and swiftly dealt with protection.

"Time for me to ravish you," he told the petite woman who'd done a masterful job of pushing him to the edge. Then his hands and mouth got to work, winning him quiet murmurs, then outright moans, until at last he pulled her under him and sank into her with one sure thrust. Oh, yeah, he thought. This was where he wanted to be. Craved to be.

Had to be.

It was Amanda's turn to draw in a ragged breath. As always, the sensations he could produce deep inside her threatened her ability to think. And she wanted to think, wanted to remember every detail of making love with him this time.

Because this time was different.

She wasn't sure how she knew that, she only knew she did. Perhaps it was because they'd opened up to each other and shared some confidences tonight—confidences of the most private and personal kind. Perhaps that was it.

One thing for certain, as she'd expected, it hadn't been easy to reveal those facts about her father. Still, she had no regrets, even though it somehow made their joining now seem more intimate in a way that could pose a threat to more than her capacity to think. It could, in fact, put her resolve to guard her emotions where this man was concerned in danger.

Don't let yourself be swayed too much by what he

can make you feel, the voice of reason said, and she couldn't ignore the wisdom of those words.

But oh, he felt so good. So right.

So…special.

"Are you following me here?" Dev asked, his voice a rough whisper at her ear.

For some reason, that made her grin. "I'm right behind you."

He picked up the pace, rapidly increasing the rhythm of their mutual movements. "Time to close the gap."

"It's closing," she said, her grin fading as something began to tighten in her most secret places. Her breath quickened. Her heart thumped.

His own heart thundered against his ribs as he pressed his chest to her breasts, flattening her against the mattress. "I want you screaming when it hits."

"I can't," she got out on a quiet gasp. "I'll wake up Betsy."

"No, you won't." His lips moved to cover hers. "Scream into my mouth."

And, in a matter of moments, she did exactly that as everything inside her seemed to burst into a million pieces.

He swallowed her sharp cry, then picked up the pace yet again, until he stiffened at last and shuddered in her arms. And now she was the one who swallowed his low shout before he collapsed on top of her.

She took his weight without complaint and just held on with all her might. Their bodies were fused together in the aftermath of spent passion, but their joining went beyond that, she sensed. As strange as it seemed, it was almost as though he were a part of her, and she a part of him.

Yes, this time had been different, she thought. She still didn't know why. She only knew it was.

LITTLE BY LITTLE, Dev returned to the present. With his eyes still closed, he rolled over with a secure grip on Amanda until she again rested on top of him.

Better, he decided. Now she could breathe and he could revisit the considerable comforts of having her stretched out over him. He raised a hand and ran it down her hair. The more he saw it left free to flow over her shoulders, the more the sight pleased him. Maybe he'd hide every one of those fancy clips she owned so she couldn't keep it tied back. Uh-huh. That plan held definite appeal.

Amanda stirred. "We probably should get some sleep," she murmured.

"Yeah," he agreed. Trouble was, he had little desire to drift off yet. Right now, he was content to enjoy the moment. There hadn't been many times in his life when he'd felt this good, he realized. Could be he'd never felt this good. Again he had to admit that he owed it to the woman he was coming to like more and more as time passed.

Could be you're even starting to do more than like her, Devlin, an inner voice told him, winning his full attention.

More than like her? Dev slowly opened his eyes as that thought rolled through him. He found Amanda gazing down at him, her elbows propped on his chest and a sleepy expression on her face, as though she were ready to slide into her dreams.

He wanted to be in those dreams—and not just tonight, he recognized as the blunt truth of the matter hit him with the impact of a fist to the gut. No, he wanted a lot more than that. Needed it, in fact. And all because, unless everything inside him was badly mistaken, something was happening to him that had never happened before.

"Are you all right?" she whispered with a sudden frown.

He knew he was staring, but he couldn't help it. "I think," he told her with simple directness, "that I'm falling in love with you."

Her whole body stiffened in a flash as her eyes went wide. Then another frown appeared and dug deep into her brow as she frankly stared at him in return.

Obviously, he thought, she wasn't rejoicing at the news.

"You can't mean that," she said at last.

For some reason his temper threatened to surface, but he kept a lid on it. "I mean it."

She gave her head a quick shake. "No, it's too soon to even be considering something like that."

"I didn't consider it," he informed her in a candid admission. "It just seems to be happening."

She pulled away and rolled off him, then reached down and tugged the white top sheet up to her shoulders. "You've been through a lot today. You may think otherwise in the morning."

"I doubt it," he replied, and meant it. He didn't bother to cover himself as he turned on his side and propped his head on an upraised palm. "Mind telling me why you look so shook up?"

She hesitated for so long that he began to suspect she might not answer at all before she spoke. "This was supposed to be a different sort of marriage."

"And then things changed when we wound up in bed that first time," he reminded her.

"Yes," she allowed, "but they didn't change entirely. We just found out that we were good together, ah, physically."

He was starting to get her drift. "So we can sleep with each other, but getting in too deep in other ways could wind up being a problem, is that it?"

Again she hesitated. "It could be a major problem," she told him, her voice soft yet as serious as he'd ever heard it, "if the marriage doesn't last."

That had been their agreement, he had no trouble recalling. Once she had full legal custody of her sisters and brothers, the two of them would be free to go their separate ways whenever they chose to down the road. But that was before they'd lived together. And slept together. And shared some private details about themselves and their families.

"What makes you think the marriage might not last?" he had to ask.

A quiet sigh broke from her throat. "I'd rather not get into that. It's late and we both need some rest."

He had to wonder why she was skirting the issue. Avoiding it wasn't likely to do either of them any good. "We'll both rest easier if we get a few things straight, trust me."

But she didn't trust him.

Dev drew in a sharp breath, suddenly as certain of that as he was of his own name. And, unless he'd gone flat around the bend, it all went back to what had happened with her parents.

Amanda cleared her throat delicately. "I think it would be better to—"

He broke in, deciding to cut to the chase. "You're worried that I won't be there for you any more than your father turned out to be there for your mother, aren't you?''

The stark seconds of dead silence that followed told him he was on the right track. Damn, he thought grimly, he didn't want to be right. Not this time.

"I'm not the gambler he was. Throwing a buck a week into the lottery pool has basically been my limit. But I was wild enough in other ways at one time to have you questioning whether I'd be a good bet to stick around for the long haul." He paused for a beat. "Your mother found out that it was risky to rely on your father—and now you're leery of taking a chance on me."

More silence greeted those words. Again that was enough to tell him what he didn't want to know. "I could say you're wrong, that I really have changed. But it all boils down to the fact that if you can't trust me enough to take chance on me," he added as he shifted and got out of bed, "then this marriage probably doesn't have much hope of making it."

He'd pulled on his jeans and had started for the door to the hall in his bare feet before the sound of Amanda's quiet voice drifted over his shoulder.

"Where are you going?"

He didn't turn around. "I'm not much of a drinking man anymore these days, either," he said, "but a beer seems to be in order. Lord knows, it's been one helluva day."

And with that, he walked out.

HE'D READ HER like a book. In fact, he'd given her a whole new awareness of why she'd been so reluctant to believe he would ever really settle down. The father she'd adored had abandoned both her and her mother, and although her mother had bounced back and met the challenge of living life without him, her daughter had never been able to quite wipe out what had happened in the past. Dev Devlin had been right about that, Amanda thought, just as he'd been right about something else.

If she couldn't find it in her heart to truly trust her husband, they could never have a real future together.

Nearly a week had passed since the memorable night he'd made that plain to her in no uncertain terms, and she was still far from certain where they went from here. At home, they'd both managed to act as though everything was fine for the children's sake. Away from the house, they'd continued their project of making some improvements to the Heartbreaker. At night, they still slept together in the same bed. They'd even silently turned to each other for physical satisfaction more than once in the quiet hours between midnight and dawn.

But, despite all of that, everything was far from fine, she knew.

"You need to perk up," Irene Caldwell said, taking a break from her investigation of the large carton holding the latest shipment of books that had arrived at the Ex-Libris. As usual, the avid reader had been eager to inspect the new stock. "In case you hadn't noticed, it's a beautiful afternoon."

Amanda ignored the older woman's abruptly probing look and summoned a smile. "That it is," she agreed with determined good cheer.

Like any veteran Montana resident, she wouldn't have been all that surprised to find a late snowstorm in progress as she glanced out the store's wide front window. Instead, spring in all its warm and sun-splashed glory had chosen to come out and play. If the good weather lasted, before long wild flowers could well be blooming in the meadows outside town.

Irene went back to her investigation. "Some of these books look as old as the hills. Finn Hollis must have ordered them. I don't think he's ever going to stop."

"The scholarly man would probably refer to them as rare first editions in prime shape," Amanda countered. She took another short sip of the frothy mocha she'd slipped over to the diner for earlier. Sometimes tea just didn't do it.

"Well, they're still as old as the hills, rare or not." With that verdict, Irene straightened a second before Stella Montgomery walked in from the street.

Amanda set her drink down on the counter. Her smile reappeared as she offered a greeting. When it came to Jester's older population, she felt closest to Finn and Irene, probably because they shared an abiding love for the written word. Still, she had always liked Stella, too. Then again, how could you not like someone who looked like a merry cherub with her tight blond curls and slightly pudgy figure?

"Thought I'd find you here," Stella told Irene. Both women lived at the boarding house and were fast friends. "I just got the urge for a hot fudge sundae. Want to join me in consuming some calories?"

Irene mulled that over for a moment, then nodded. "Why not? It'll be a while yet to dinner."

"We'll have a new boarder at the supper table tonight." Stella, who liked meeting people, was obviously pleased.

"Man or woman?" Irene asked.

"Woman. She didn't say much when she checked

in a few minutes ago.'' A thoughtful expression settled on Stella's face. ''I seem to remember seeing her in Jester before. She was driving the same blue sedan she parked at the boarding house today.''

Irene frowned. ''Not a reporter, is she?''

''Oh, I don't think so.'' Stella tapped a small finger to her lips. ''Although I suspect she'd be a tough interviewer. She has a let's-get-down-to-business air about her. You know, the no-nonsense type.''

Those last words won Amanda's notice. She knew someone who would fit that description, she mused to herself after bidding Irene and Stella goodbye. Someone, she recalled, who drove a blue sedan. Someone, in fact, who was no stranger to Jester.

No, she was letting her imagination take over, she thought. It couldn't be *her.*

Then, in the next breath, she discovered it *was* her as the front door opened again and Louise Pearson stepped in.

''Hello,'' Amanda said from her place behind the counter. She considered trying to dredge up a smile, but Louise looked far from ready to offer one in return. Her expression was as sober as Amanda had ever seen it.

''Good afternoon,'' the social worker replied in her typical brisk fashion. ''Would your husband be next door at this time of day?''

That question, issued without the barest of preliminaries, brought Amanda up short. It took her a moment to respond. ''Yes, he should be at the Heartbreaker.''

''Good.'' Louise dipped her chin in a satisfied nod. ''I would appreciate it if you could ask him to join us.

I'd like to talk to you both, and I'd rather not do it at your home, where the children may be around.''

A shiver of unease ran down Amanda's spine. "Is something wrong?"

"That remains to be seen," Louise told her.

Amanda reached for the phone behind the counter and punched in the saloon's number. It rang twice before the call was picked up on the other end.

"Heartbreaker. Devlin here."

"It's Amanda," she told him. "Can you come over to the store right away?"

"Sure," he replied after a brief pause. It was plain that he hadn't expected that request. "Everything okay?"

Amanda ignored that question in favor of a short explanation. "Louise Pearson is here and she'd like to talk to the both of us."

Another pause, longer this time, followed. "Is that good or bad?" he asked at last.

"I wish I knew," she murmured.

"Be right there."

Amanda carefully replaced the receiver. "Why don't we make ourselves comfortable in the sitting area at the back?" She gestured the way with a lifted hand.

"All right," Louise replied. She marched off toward the rear of the store and took a seat on one of the leather chairs.

Amanda followed. "Can I fix you a cup of tea?"

"No, thank you."

So much for the social graces, Amanda thought. She sank down on a love seat and folded her hands in her lap, glad that she'd chosen to wear her cream-colored wool suit on this particular Friday. At least she was on the same footing as her visitor, who'd opted for another strictly business outfit.

Louise didn't seem inclined to make casual conversation, so Amanda kept her peace and counted the seconds until the front door opened and closed. A few long strides brought Dev to the back of the bookstore.

He took a seat beside Amanda and only the barest greetings were exchanged before Louise sat forward. "Since I'm sure you're curious as to why I requested this meeting, I won't waste any time getting to the point." She switched her penetrating gaze back and forth to include both of the Devlins. "An anonymous source has contacted Child and Family Services and made some interesting claims."

Interesting claims? Amanda was wondering what that could possibly mean when Louise continued.

"According to the information received, the two of you were longstanding adversaries before your hasty marriage. In fact, you were seen engaging in more than one confrontation outside your respective businesses."

The fingers Amanda had laced together tightened. Her first impulse, one born of desperation when she considered how that information might affect her sisters and brothers, was to flatly deny what she'd just been told. Then reason kicked in and she realized that it might be far wiser to try to put the best possible slant on what was, after all, the truth.

As though he'd reached the same conclusion, Dev said, "Well, it wasn't always easy operating a bookstore and a bar next to each other, but our differences weren't near as serious as this *anonymous source* might have figured." His voice took on a hard-as-steel edge at the reference to whoever had contacted Family Services.

Amanda frowned. Was it the same person who had leaked information to the media about the private lives of some of the Main Street Millionaires following the lottery win? she wondered. She had to conclude that it could well be.

"So your differences weren't serious?" Louise asked, arching a meaningful brow. There was no mistaking the suspicion glinting in her gaze.

"Not by any means," Amanda informed her, making that as firm a statement as she could.

Louise mulled that over for a second. "And your getting married was a love match, pure and simple?"

"Absolutely," Dev wasted no time in replying. To back that up, he laid an arm around Amanda's shoulders. "I explained how it was at our meeting in Pine Run."

"Yes, you did," Louise agreed dryly, as though she had little trouble recalling how persuasive he'd been. "And at the time, of course, there was nothing on record to dispute it. Now, however, this new information will have to be checked out. Which I intend to do," she added with a determined look, "very thoroughly."

"I'll bet you will," Dev said in a low murmur just loud enough for Amanda to catch.

"In the meantime," Louise told them as she rose to her feet, "the petition for adoption of the Bradley children has been put on hold pending the results of my findings."

Amanda felt a momentary panic that threatened to swamp her. Surely the children wouldn't be taken away from her. The authorities had to recognize that where they were was the best place for them. They had to. She wanted to believe that so badly it helped her maintain an outer layer of calm. When the man beside dropped his arm from her shoulders and stood in one rapid motion, she followed his example and viewed their visitor with a small lift of her chin.

"We'll be waiting to hear from you," she told Louise.

The two women traded a long look before Louise issued a final statement. "I'll be staying at the local boarding house for a few days while I gather more facts, so I should be able to come to some conclusions soon." With that, she turned and started for the front of the store, leaving the Devlins to look after her as she departed.

The door had barely closed behind the social worker when Dev issued a ripe curse. "If I ever find out who that anonymous source was, they won't be happy, believe me."

Amanda believed him. There was no mistaking the gritty resolve in his deep voice. "The question is," she said on a sigh, "what can we do to make sure Louise's findings are favorable?"

"At the moment I'm in more of a mood to kick some butt," he bit out.

She looked up at him. "I wouldn't mind kicking some myself."

That earned her a faint smile. "Well, you're not all that big, but you're mighty, I've got to admit."

She couldn't quite manage a smile in return at a concession she once would have never expected to win, certainly not from the person whose tight male backside she'd wanted to put a well-placed foot to more than a time or two in the past. "The thing is, kicking whatever might fill the bill, as satisfying as it may be in the short term, won't get us anywhere."

He blew out a resigned breath and shoved the hands that had been fisted at his sides into his jeans pockets. "Too bad I have to concede that you're right on that score."

"The question is, what can we do that might get us somewhere?" she asked, sharing his clear frustration. "We can't stop Louise from gathering information about us, and we can't stop people in Jester from providing it."

"I can close a few mouths if I have to."

She rolled her eyes. "No kicking or closing any part of anyone's anatomy, okay?"

He shrugged. "Okay, if you want to ruin all my fun."

"There has to be another way." She paused for a thoughtful beat. "Unfortunately the only thing I can come up with at the moment is to try to put the best face possible on whatever Louise learns. And even to do that much we'll probably need some help," she acknowledged. "Maybe a lot of help."

"Well," he said after a second's consideration, "between the two of us we have more than a few friends in town."

Her spirits took a slight shift for the better. "Yes, and at least some of them are sure to be willing to help us." She longed to reach out and touch him, longed for a comforting touch in return. Instead she held back, mindful of the fact that although they continued to turn to each other in the middle of the night, they remained far from the happily wedded couple they'd gone out of their way to present to the rest of the world.

But this wasn't the time to think about that, she told herself. Right now the most important thing was to join forces yet again with the man she'd married to convince the authorities once and for all that her sisters and brothers should remain with her, safely and permanently.

She had to hope against hope they would be successful.

Chapter Twelve

Dev fired up the grill on a sunny Sunday afternoon. It was another beautiful May day, warm enough for the kids to play outside without a jacket on. The backyard grass was sprouting up, providing a good spot for them to tumble around in their bright T-shirts and light-weight pants.

Patrick wore his straw cowboy hat, one he hadn't let stray far from his head since he'd first put it on. Caleb had taken a shine to his baseball cap, as well. Liza was showing her brothers how to do a cartwheel without falling on their face while Betsy babbled to the birds chirping up a storm in the trees. The whole bunch was having a fine time enjoying the great out-doors, Dev thought.

Too bad he wasn't.

Forty-eight hours had passed without so much as a word from Louise Pearson on what she'd been able to dig up on him and Amanda. As a result, they still had little clue as to what was in store for them—or the kids. And the waiting was getting to him, he had to admit.

Rufus hopped down from his perch on the deck rail-ing and stalked over to rub himself against Dev's denim-clad legs. "I suppose you'd like me to think you're trying to raise my spirits," he muttered, dropping a look down at the cat, "but you don't fool me, pal. You're cozying up to me because I'm about to burn some hot dogs and sweet sausage for lunch."

A loud purr greeted that statement.

"Yeah, yeah. Tell it to someone you didn't throw over for a pretty young face."

Amanda stepped through the sliding glass doors to the kitchen carrying a large platter covered with tin foil. She was dressed almost as casually as the kids in a V-necked sweater and khakis. Still, she wasn't nearly as rosy-cheeked as her sisters and brothers, Dev noted.

Not that she hadn't put up a cheerful front for them. She had. They didn't see the growing worry in her eyes when she watched them having a good time just being young and carefree. But he saw plenty.

The waiting was getting to her, too.

"Here's the hot dogs and sausage." She set the platter down on the shelf jutting out from one side of the gas grill.

"Just make sure you eat your share," he told her. He hadn't missed the fact that her appetite was a long way from normal. "No just shoving the food around on your plate and pretending that you ate a real meal."

She didn't deny it. She simply looked up at him and arched a brow. "I'm beginning to think you're nearly as sharp-eyed as a certain social worker we both know."

He thought about trying out a smile, then decided against it, figuring it would be a halfhearted effort at best. "Why don't you forget about her for a while?"

Amanda's expression sobered in a heartbeat. "I can't."

"Then try remembering that we've got some friends on our side," he told her, knowing the truth of that. He and Amanda had wasted no time in telling Shelly O'Rourke the details behind Louise Pearson's visit to Jester, and the Brimming Cup's owner had promised to quietly pass the word along to the rest of their friends.

We won't let you down. That's what Shelly had said, Dev recalled, not for the first time. It had helped him resist the urge to slam a frustrated fist into the wall more than once during the past two days.

"You're right," Amanda conceded. "Thank God for friends. I just wish I knew whether they've been able to accomplish anything. I tried to call Shelly a little while ago and there was no answer at her place."

Just then the cordless phone on the deck's redwood table rang. Amanda made a beeline for it and picked it up. "Shelly—" she started to say. A short silence followed before she spoke again. "But what—" Frowning, she set the phone down.

Dev found himself frowning in return. "Was it Shelly?"

She shook her head. "No, it was Roy Gibson. He said the two of us have to get over to the Heartbreaker right away. Then he hung up."

He couldn't figure that one out. "The bar's not even open on Sunday."

Concern clouded her gaze. "It sounded urgent."

That news prompted some concern of his own. His head bartender wasn't a man to get riled up over anything less than a real emergency. "All right, I'll go and you can stay here with the kids."

"Roy stressed that we both had to come." She picked up the phone again. "I'll call Mabel and see if she can watch the children."

But the Murphys didn't answer, any more than Shelly had earlier. "I guess we'll just have to take them with us," Dev said. He could only be thankful that Amanda had already made some changes at the saloon. At least the two ripe beauties on the wall behind the bar, now covered with some fancy lace, wouldn't have the kids' eyes popping out of their heads.

With a quick nod, she hurried over and grabbed up the food platter. "I'll put this in the refrigerator while you turn off the grill."

He switched off the burners and bent to twist the gauge on the gas tank shut, then straightened and called to the kids. "Lunch is going to be late today, guys. We have to go over to the Heartbreaker for a little while."

The boys came running up to him. "We get to see where you work?" Caleb asked with clear enthusiasm.

"That's right."

"Can I wear my hat?" Patrick wanted to know.

"No place better to wear it," Dev told him. "The Heartbreaker's seen more than its share of cowboys."

Betsy toddled toward him, her grin as jolly as the one displayed by the cartoon elephant on her yellow shirt. Liza followed, decked out in cheery pink and looking as eager as her brothers to inspect a spot they'd only seen from the outside.

They all trooped into the house together. The house, Dev reflected as he locked the sliding door behind them, that he'd built with only himself in mind and that was now home to a family. It was hard to imagine living there by himself anymore. Which could happen, he knew, if things didn't work out.

Not that he was anywhere near prepared to concede defeat when it came to the gut-wrenching prospect of seeing four towheads being taken away by the authorities. *We won't let you down.* He was determined to keep that promise in mind. It hadn't been made lightly, he recognized, and he had to count on the Devlins' friends to make good on it.

But even if the kids stayed in Jester and the adoption went through, he could well still wind up living alone.

"Ready to go?" Amanda asked.

"Yeah, I'm ready." *Ready to be a father to the kids and a husband to you in every way that matters,* he added silently. *Ready to be a man who looks forward to coming home to his family night after night as the years go by. Ready to start being one half of a real, true-blue, happily married couple...and never stopping.*

Trouble was, the odds against any of that happening were zilch as long as his wife doubted his sticking power.

Dev grabbed his Stetson from the hall closet and left the house with Amanda at his side, thinking that it was just his bad luck that he'd been wrong when he'd told her he thought he was falling in love with her. He no longer thought it. He flat-out *knew* it.

And now he might have to watch her walk out of his life.

"Main Street isn't usually this quiet," Amanda said. "There's not a soul in sight." Then again, she reflected as she glanced around her, on the evening she'd met trouble in the form of a burly drunk bent on giving her a major problem to deal with, no one had been around to come to her aid. No one, that is, except the man currently seated beside her.

So maybe it wasn't so unusual to find Main Street empty, but this was a gorgeous day, the kind not common enough at this time of year to be taken for granted. With that in mind, she couldn't deny it seemed odd to see the street deserted.

Dev headed the minivan toward the saloon. "At least there's no commotion outside the Heartbreaker. Whatever Roy considered urgent, it hasn't led to a mob scene."

He parked the van in front of his business and came around the passenger's side to help get the children out. Hoisting the littlest of the group into his arms, he brought up the rear as Amanda started across the sidewalk with the older children. They were steps from the corner entrance to the saloon when she came to a sudden halt.

"You know," Amanda said, glancing back at her husband, "I have the strangest feeling that something's going on."

He arched a brow. "What do you mean, a feeling?"

"I'm not sure what I mean exactly," she had to concede. She didn't know why a small voice seemed to be telling her that everything wasn't as it appeared to be. She only knew what she heard in the back of her mind.

"Women's intuition?" he asked with a wry slant of his lips.

She hesitated. "Maybe."

"Well, let's go in and see if there's anything to it."

That sounded so reasonable, she could hardly object. The heavy door kept locked when the Heart-breaker was closed now stood open, she noted, again moving forward. Only the swinging doors were shut. They creaked a greeting as she slowly stepped inside. And then a chorus of shouts broke out, melding into a single word.

"Surprise!"

Amanda's mouth gaped open as she stared at the crowd crammed into the saloon. It seemed as if half of Jester's citizens were looking back at her with wide smiles. At last she found her voice. "What in the world is going on?"

"It must be a surprise birthday party," Caleb offered from beside her. "I went to one once when I was little."

Shelly laughed and stepped forward. "Well, you're certainly not little anymore," she told the five-year-old. Then she raised her sparking gaze to include the rest of the new arrivals. "As it happens, though, this is a surprise wedding."

A surprise wedding. Amanda was still trying to grasp the implications of that statement when the crowd parted down the center and she saw that the saloon had been decorated with flowers in all colors, shapes and sizes. Its long oak bar now held a lengthy buffet filled with food, and the star attraction was a three-tiered cake with creamy white frosting.

"But who's getting mar—" she started to ask. Then she spotted the large, hand-lettered sign draped high over the small wooden stage at the rear of the room, where a five-man country band was assembled.

"Congratulations, Amanda and Dev," she murmured, reading the sign out loud.

"Well, I'll be dam—darned," a low voice offered from behind her.

She glanced back to find her husband looking every bit as amazed as she was. Even Betsy, still held securely in his arms, was studying the scene before her with wide eyes.

"That's right," Shelly told Dev with mock censure, "you need to mind your language." Then she reached out and caught Amanda in an enthusiastic hug. "I told you weddings should be a big deal."

"So you did," was the only response Amanda could manage at the moment.

"And the women at the boarding house have made sure that Mrs. Pearson is here to take it all in," Shelly added, dropping her voice to a whisper. "Your friends are going to show her that we think your marriage is more than romantic enough to deserve two weddings."

Amanda aimed a sweeping look over her friend's shoulder and found the social worker standing off to one side of the room between Irene and Stella. Where everyone else seemed to be casually dressed for the occasion in a mixture of Western-style wear and colorful cotton dresses, shirts and pants, Louise wore a tailored navy suit. Her narrowed stare said she was assessing the situation.

Amanda sighed. "I just hope it works."

"Keep a good thought," Shelly advised before pulling back. "Now it's time to get this show on the road. I'm offering my services as matron of honor, by the way."

Amanda found her lips curving despite concerns about the future that refused to fade. "You've got the job."

Finn Hollis, wearing one of his tweed jackets and looking scholarly even with a saloon as a backdrop, stepped forward. "I'm prepared to give the bride away, if she'll have me."

She couldn't think of anyone in Jester who would better suit her. "I'll have you," she didn't hesitate to tell him.

"Good." Shelly linked her arm with Amanda's. "Let's head to the ladies' room and put the final touches on your outfit."

Amanda dropped a look down at her ivory sweater, khaki slacks and tan loafers. "If I'd had any inkling that you were going to spring this on me, I would have at least worn a dress."

"I told everyone this would be a come-as-you-are wedding," Shelly informed her as they started across the room. "If my expanding waistline wasn't making it more and more difficult to close the zipper of my jeans, I would have come that way, believe me. As it is, I had to settle for a roomier outfit if I wanted to be comfortable."

Gwen Tanner waved a greeting as they passed her. Like Shelly, the boarding-house owner and avid baker wore a lightweight floral-print dress with a loose waistline. Unlike Shelly, however, the identity of the man who had gotten Gwen pregnant remained a mystery.

"You made the cake, didn't you?" Amanda called out.

Gwen smiled her sweet smile. "Guilty as charged."

Amanda and Shelly entered the restroom and found Sylvia Rutledge waiting for them. The tall, slim and always stylish blonde who operated the Crowning Glory hair salon had plainly had no trouble donning a

pair of snug designer jeans that were a fitting match
for her fashionable turquoise-and-silver striped blouse.
She held a short length of gauzy white fabric topped
with a circle of fresh flowers in one of her well-
manicured hands.

"Even if it this is a come-as-you-are wedding," she
told Amanda with a sly grin, "we decided the bride
needed a veil."

"And while Sylvia's putting it on, I have to get your
wedding ring and give it to the best man," Shelly said.
"Which should be Roy unless Dev turns him down
flat for hauling the two of you over here with that
trumped-up phone call."

Amanda pulled off her plain gold ring and handed
it to Shelly. "I'll keep my engagement ring."

Sylvia laughed softly as Shelly left. "I would, too,
if I had a rock like that."

"I never expected to have it," Amanda admitted,
dipping her gaze to the elegantly cut diamond. "But
you can afford to buy one." She knew the truth of
that, since Sylvia was another of the big lottery winners.

The woman who seemed to enjoy her single status
shook her head. "That's not the kind of ring a female
buys for herself. Takes a man to do it right. Now, let
me get to work."

MINUTES LATER, to the tune of "Here Comes the
Bride" skillfully played on a lone fiddle, Amanda
walked down a makeshift aisle on one of Finn's lanky
arms with her long hair swept up off her neck and her
veil brushing the small of her back. It was so different
from the first time, she thought, recalling the earlier
ceremony conducted in the judge's chambers. This

time there were mounds of flowers, a beautiful wedding cake and a sea of friendly faces.

Even some much-loved faces, she could hardly deny, catching sight of the children who watched her with clear wonder in their eyes. A beaming Mabel, looking as pleased as punch with her part in surprising the couple next door, now held Betsy while the three older members of the Bradley bunch stood next to the part-time nanny and her equally beaming spouse.

"Mandeee!" Betsy called out, waving one tiny hand.

Amanda waved back, deciding that this time wasn't only different, but far better in many ways.

Nevertheless, something remained the same, she realized as she continued to take measured steps toward the rear of the saloon and recognized the big, broad-shouldered judge who awaited her at the foot of the stage that held the band. Today Judge Corbett looked more like a rancher than a court official in his Wranglers and leather vest, but the large smile he offered as she came to a halt in front of him was unmistakably familiar.

"Nice to see you again, little lady." He tipped his wide-brimmed hat in greeting. "I'm glad you didn't keep the groom waiting too long. He had the look of a raring-to-go male who wants to get hitched pronto as he watched you walk down the aisle. Probably," the judge added, cocking a bushy brow, "so he can get started on kissing the bride one more time."

Finn patted her hand. "I'm guessing His Honor is right," he remarked with a low chuckle before stepping back.

Amanda slowly turned her head and looked at the man she'd deliberately avoided so much as a glance at for the last few minutes, the man who was about to become her husband yet again. The same man who stood next to his head bartender and stared at her from under the rim of his Stetson with a resolute set of his chiseled jaw, as though determined to do something come hell or high water. But what? she wondered.

Then she found out in the next breath when he broke with tradition and reached out to pull her to him in one swift motion. Before she could so much as blink, he lowered his head and brought his lips to her ear.

"You may not want to hear it," he said in a rough whisper, "but I have to say my piece. This time, I want it to be the real thing, Amanda. A *real* love match, not a sham one. That's why, even though the odds might be against me, I'm dead-set on asking you here and now to take a chance and trust me when I swear that I mean to spend the rest of my life with you."

She felt the tension holding his body rigid, felt her pulse begin to leap in response. He'd meant every word he'd said. There was no mistaking the clear ring of truth in his voice. He really did intend to spend the rest of his life with her. But would those intentions slip away as time went by?

She would never know unless she took him at his word and simply believed. That was crux of the matter, of course. She had to believe in him.

And not only in him, she suddenly recognized. She had to believe in both of them and what they could have together. She had to believe in his ability to settle down for a lifetime, and in her ability to put fears arising from past events aside and trust him, day after day, year after year, no matter what they might face in the future.

When in doubt, do what your heart tells you, the grandmother she'd adored as a very young child used to say.

And what did hers say right now? Reaching deep down inside herself, Amanda listened with all her might…and learned.

"Yes, I'm willing to take a chance," she whispered back. "On you. On us. And on the fact that my heart is telling me that I love you."

Dev let out a surge of air. Until that moment, he hadn't realized he'd been holding his breath. Watching his wife walk down that aisle, looking everywhere but at him, he'd known he had to try to make things right between them, no matter what the outcome. So he'd taken a risk that would affect the rest of his life—and, thank God, he'd netted himself the role of family man.

Pulling back, he gazed down at Amanda. "Sweetheart, you won't regret it."

Her lips curved at the tips. "No, I don't believe I will."

He glanced at the judge, then back at the woman in his arms. "I think we're ready to start the ceremony."

"All right. Would you folks like to go with the same traditional vows the second time around, or just say what you feel this time?"

Amanda looked straight into her husband's eyes. "I think we should let everyone here know how we feel."

Dev swallowed. Despite his reputation as a sweet-talker, he'd never made any fancy speeches. And he didn't have to now, something in the back of his mind told him. All he had to do was put one word in front of the other, and if he spoke the plain, unvarnished truth, it would be the best speech he'd ever made.

So he gave Amanda the words that came from gut-deep inside him, and she in turn told him what was in her heart. And as they declared their love for each other, loudly and proudly, more than a few sniffles could be heard in the background before rings were once again exchanged and the judge declared them husband and wife. Then the groom kissed the bride, slowly and thoroughly, as the crowd issued a loud cheer worthy of the Heartbreaker's longstanding status as the rowdiest spot in town.

"Don't I get to kiss the bride, too?" the best man asked at last. "I got all gussied up for this shindig, you know."

Roy's idea of "gussied up" was to wear a string tie with his faded Western garb, Dev thought with amusement as he let the older man have his way. It wasn't long before he found himself being kissed by the matron of honor.

"Aren't you glad we surprised you?" Shelly asked.

"You don't know the half of it," Dev replied.

Connor O'Rourke, minus his doctor's uniform today, walked up and put an arm around Shelly's waist. "Just don't make a habit of kissing my wife, okay?"

Dev tucked his tongue in his teeth. "I'll try not to."

"For the moment," Shelly said, "he'll be too busy obliging a whole bunch of other females."

And he was. Enthusiastic kisses from the women in attendance and hearty handshakes from the men followed. After which Dev pulled the bride away from yet another man bent on kissing her and got in a second one for himself. He wasn't even aware that Louise Pearson had stepped up beside them before she spoke.

"Congratulations. That was a lovely ceremony," the social worker remarked, sounding as though she truly meant it.

Was that a hint of a stray tear in her eyes? Dev asked himself, studying her. Nah, it couldn't be.

"We're glad you enjoyed it," Amanda said.

"I have no intention of keeping you from your celebration," Louise told them. "I simply wanted you to know what I just witnessed has convinced me of your sincerity. If yours isn't a love match, I don't think I've ever seen one."

"Does that mean…?" Dev let the question hang.

She nodded. "Yes, I'm recommending that the petition for adoption be allowed to proceed."

He slanted a look at Amanda and saw pure relief swiftly followed by sheer joy displayed on her face. In the next breath, she was hugging Louise. "Thank you."

The social worker hugged her back. "Do you suppose I could get a kiss from the groom?"

"You bet," Dev assured her. And then he made good on his word, in spades.

"Oh, my," Louise said when he let her up for air.

He resisted the devilish urge to do it again for good measure and settled for offering his own thanks as Mabel and Ike walked over with the kids in tow. "They were jumping up and down with excitement when the judge declared you two married for a second time," Mabel told the Devlins.

Amanda bent and hugged all of the children soundly. Dev exchanged man-to-man handshakes with Caleb and Patrick and dropped a brief, smacking kiss down on a smiling Liza's cheek. Then it was Betsy's turn to win his attention as she left Amanda's side and toddled over to him.

"Up, Deveee!"

He nearly winced. He'd gotten used to hearing her call him that, but not in front of an audience. Lifting her into his arms, he aimed a glance at several men who stood close by. Dean Kenning, who'd abandoned his barber smock in favor of a red shirt bright enough to make a person blink, was plainly trying to swallow a laugh and barely succeeding. Luke McNeil, usually every inch the tall, dark and stalwart sheriff, coughed into his hand to hide a grin—and failed. And Dev's own best man was obviously on the verge of letting out a howl.

Don't give me any grief over this, Dev told them with a silent stare. Then he looked at the little girl he held. "Do I get a kiss, your majesty?"

She thought about it for a moment, then leaned in and pressed her tiny lips to his cheek. And that made it all worthwhile. Just like that, he didn't give a damn if anyone gave him a hard time. He was a contented man.

"Time to open the champagne!" Roy declared, finally getting a handle on himself.

"Yes," Amanda agreed, "it's time to celebrate."

Dev met her gaze across the heads of the older children as the band struck up a lively tune. "I get the first dance with you. And the last."

She smiled a knowing smile, as if she'd somehow read his mind and latched on to his newly formed plan to have their last dance take place when they were finally alone—after he carried her over the threshold and all the way up to their bedroom. "You can have as many dances as you want."

He wiggled a wicked eyebrow. "Then I'll take more than my fair share."

"I don't wanna dance," Caleb said.

"Me, neither," Patrick chimed in.

"I do," said a soft voice.

Everyone looked at Liza. "I'll be sure to take you up on that," Dev told her, "and we'll have a whopping good time. This is a special day, and we're going to make it count."

"Maybe the most special day," Amanda added. Once again her gaze locked with her husband's, and there was no mistaking the love shining in it. "After all, this is the day we found out that we're going to live happily ever after."

In the hours that followed, champagne toasts were offered and much food was consumed by many, including four towheads who had worked up enough of an appetite watching their big sister get married to eagerly request second slices of her wedding cake. People of all ages danced to their heart's content as afternoon drifted into evening, and no one seemed more content to put their feet to good use than the bride and groom. With their attention centered on each other, they seldom spared a glance around them to see how frequently heads came together as some late-breaking news began to circulate among the crowd.

The rising whispers said that Sam Cade, Ruby's estranged husband, had been seen in town. And that was news, indeed.

"Wonder where he's been," Finn remarked to Dean as the two men stood at the edge of the dance floor.

"I've got to wonder how long it'll be before he and Ruby have it out about some things," the barber replied. "Doesn't seem as though a military man would just stand by and let her divorce him if he decides he wants his wife.''

Finn studied the two people who had brought so many of Jester's residents to the Heartbreaker that day. ''Well, if Dev Devlin and Amanda Bradley with all their differences can make a marriage work, I suppose anything's possible.''

''Yep,'' Dean said. ''I guess that's right.'' As the newlyweds glided by, he called out to them. ''Looks like you can thank your lucky stars, Dev, that a real lady decided to take you on!''

Dev grinned from ear-to-ear. ''That's something Amanda and I won't ever argue about!'' he called back. Then he lifted the woman in his arms right off her feet and waltzed her around in a wide circle, just as he had on the snowy night he'd become a Main Street Millionaire.

Only this time, he didn't let her go.

* * * * *

*Find out what happens when one
of the Main Street Millionaires
is reunited with her long lost husband
in the next installment of*
MILLIONAIRE, MONTANA.
Don't miss

PRICELESS MARRIAGE

*by Bonnie Gardner, available in May 2003.
Only from Harlequin American Romance*

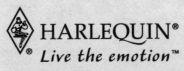

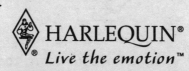

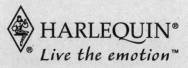